WE RETURN TO THE PROGRAM
NOW IN PROGRESS

And while we here at *All Access* have been calling it a wardrobe malfunction, in a statement released today Eesha tells us, "No, it was supposed to do that."

All Access regrets the error.

Now our top story! "Family Secrets and Secret Families"! Reggie Dwight's back in the news again with revelations that he has a *son and daughter* and was married briefly before changing his name!

HOST

Reggie hasn't been seen since his recent televised meeting with Queen Elizabeth II, during which he once again assaulted the monarch and claimed that she's an imposter working for the Goodco Cereal Company as part of an alleged plan to rule the earth!

KNIGHT IN WHINING ARMOR?

KNIGHT IN WHINING ARMOR?

Sources say this video shows Reggie getting assistance from a tiny man and a fire-breathing bird! Supernatural allies or a little movie magic? The jury's still out, but drummer and pop star Sir Richard Starkey is ready to pass judgment on the man he once called friend.

Reggie was keeping company with an...odd group. Including his son and daughter, apparently.

They told me this fairy tale about... well, fairies. Said the fairies were killing off knights so we won't slay their pet dragon, or some bollocks.

HOST

Sir Reggie Dwight was born John Doe in the London suburbs and later moved to New York to attend NYU.

HOST

There he met a physics student named Samantha Adams, whom he married after a lengthy courtship, and they had two children, Scottish and Polly, before separating.

HOST

Samantha Doe (née Adams) couldn't be reached for this story, and it's anybody's guess where the children are.

We are pursuing every credible lead concerning the whereabouts of Sir Reggie and his group, but...

...it's like they just vanished off the face of the earth.

IDOLWILD!

HOST

Up next!

Why is this little dog "barking mad" about last night's *Idol* finale?

More after this.

CHAM
BREAK

ADAM

IPIONS
FAST

REX

BALZER + BRAY
An Imprint of HarperCollins Publishers

Also by **ADAM REX**

FAT VAMPIRE: A Never Coming of Age Story

The Cold Cereal Saga

COLD CEREAL

UNLUCKY CHARMS

Balzer + Bray is an imprint of HarperCollins Publishers.

Champions of Breakfast
Copyright © 2014 by Adam Rex

ISBN 978-0-06-206009-9

15 16 17 18 19 OPM 10 9 8 7 6 5 4 3 2 1
❖
First paperback edition, 2015

For the real Scott and Polly

PROLOGUE

The butcher and the baker sat on the grassy hilltop and watched the stranger approach through the twilight. The baker was hogging the telescope, as usual.

"He looks big," he said. "That's good. A real tall one. Bit manky lookin', maybe, but big an' strong."

"I wouldn't know," said the butcher. "He's so far away, an' here we have only the one telescope—"

"*Sh-shh!*" the baker hissed with a flick of his hand. As if he really needed it to be quiet to see. The butcher made a rude gesture behind his back.

"Blond hair . . . ," said the baker, finally. "No, wait—he's a ginger. But not a real flamin' ginger like Millie Tailor. More red-blond like Brian Smith. Shoulder length."

"Anything else?" The butcher sighed.

"Clean shaven. Sleeveless brown shirt, an' leadin' a real ugly horse. Okay, send it."

The butcher climbed up a few paces to the signal platform and swiveled it around to face the village.

Here's what you'd have seen if you were there: the butcher, standing beside a tall and sturdy tripod topped with a flat rectangle like a huge playing card balanced on its edge. It wavered a bit in the breeze and rumbled quietly like shy thunder. One side was covered nine by nine with black shutters, and as the butcher started working levers they lifted to display a pane of mirrored glass underneath. The butcher opened and closed these panels several times, all at once and then consecutively—top to bottom and bottom to top, as though tuning up for a performance. Then, with skilled fingers, he threw this lever and that, flexing only some of the shutters and then others in unmistakable patterns. He was making giant letters to be viewed by another pair of men in a tower a mile away. He spelled:

M-A-N—A-P-P-R-O-A-C-H-E-S—T-A-L-L—B-I-G—
R-E-D—B-L-O-N-D—S-H-O-U-L-D-E-R–L-E-N-G-T-H—
H-A-I-R—N-O—B-E-A-R-D—B-R-O-W-N—
S-H-I-R-T—N-O—S-L-E-E-V-E-S—U-G-L-Y—
H-O-R-S-E—W-I-L-L-I-A-M—B-A-K-E-R—I-S—
H-O-G-G-I-N-G—T-H-E—T-E-L-E-S-C-O-P-E

If you'd been there, you might have remarked that the signal machine reminded you a little of those clacking arrival/departure signs you find in old train stations—but the butcher and the baker would have had no idea what you were talking about, because this was not your world. This was Pretannica—Ireland, specifically—and the train had never been invented here. Not exactly.

The stranger thought he'd never seen a village so happy to meet new people. They'd greeted him at the gates, whisked him off to a fine public house, fed him, and plied him with drink and said the nicest things about his worthless horse. When some fairy trickery had separated him from his caravan, he'd despaired, but now this—it was like something from a story.

"And you . . . ," he stammered between drinks. "You really think I'm this . . . what did you say?"

"Chosen One," answered a smiling old man who had been introduced as Declan Sage. He was flanked by William Baker and Billy Butcher, two of the fellows from the gate. Mary Server flitted in and out of the room, bringing food and drink. The pub was otherwise empty, though there were a number of young faces pressed up against the windows outside. "I really think it," the old man added, "because you are the Chosen One. And before long you'll think it too. Billy! Bring the Scroll of Prophecy!"

The butcher hustled from the room, came back almost instantly with a long sheet of parchment secured between two tarnished bronze rods. It was spread out on the table in front of the stranger, and Declan Sage traced a wilted finger across it as he spoke.

"Centuries ago, our simple village was a happy place.

"Then the Gloria came, and the world withered and became a dusky, fairy island. And we were confined to this twilight bubble in a great black sea of nothing.

"The world continued ever so slowly to shrivel and die, and so the Fay grew angry, and then bold. They goaded the magical creatures against us and raised a dragon on the highest peak of the Black Stacks. But one day it is prophesied that a Chosen One will lead us. A stranger. And see here—it's you."

It wasn't the best likeness, maybe, but then the style was primitive. And the Chosen One was without question tall, and strong, *and look*, thought the stranger—that was his hair. That was the very shirt he was wearing. "And who's this?" asked the stranger as he pointed to another figure in full plate armor.

"That's you, after you're clothed in a fine suit of armor once worn by the great Lancelot himself at the Battle of Camlann, and waiting hollow all these centuries for the Chosen One to claim it. Then you will choose your weapons and ride up the mountain to rid this land of a smallish to moderately sized dragon."

The stranger caught his breath, and the butcher and baker exchanged glances. Declan Sage unrolled a bit more scroll to reveal the Chosen One, mounted on something of an ugly horse and stabbing a bear-sized pink dragon through the heart. The dragon's tongue lolled and its eyes rolled back in its head. The whole operation looked pretty cut-and-dry.

"Well," said the stranger. "That's not so big."

"Spoken like a real Chosen One," said the sage. "For centuries the Village of Reek has been cursed to lie in the shadow of Carrauntoohil, atop which the modestly run-of-the-mill dragon dwells."

"Village of Reek?"

"That's this village. That's where you are now."

"Nobody'd mentioned it."

"The Village of Reek has been tormented—no, why don't we say inconvenienced?—for generations by this beast. It eats our cattle, takes our children, and so forth—"

The stranger was frowning at the scroll. "Isn't the

Great Dragon Saxbriton a pink dragon?" he asked. "I thought I'd heard tell of her in these parts."

"The Great Dragon Saxbriton divides her time between a number o' different residences," said the old man briskly. "I believe she's in Cornwall this time o' year, isn't she, lads?"

"Cornwall," said William Baker.

"You cannot fail," the sage pressed. "Your victory is preordained!"

The stranger said nothing. His face was crowded with worry.

"And lo!" continued the old man with a flourish. "Also! He who slays the nameless dragon shall win the hand of fair Aife! Where is Aife?"

Billy Butcher ran out again, and returned with a smiling, ripe-skinned girl wearing a low-cut blouse.

"This is Aife Looker," said the old man, waving. "Aife Looker, Chosen One." The girl curtsied and blushed sweetly. The stranger grinned stupidly at her.

"Okay," he breathed. "I'll do it. I'll slay your dragon!"

"Excellent," said Declan Sage, and he produced another sheet of paper. "Would you mind signing this contract to that effect? There we are."

They set out at twilight. But then it was always twilight. The butcher and the baker took the stranger through

Hag's Glen and up to the Devil's Ladder that rose between Carrauntoohil and Cnoc na Péiste. There they stopped to rest, and to help the stranger into his armor, and then William Baker explained that he and Billy Butcher could go no farther, what with not being Chosen themselves.

"I . . . hope yeh win," said the butcher.

The baker shot him a look. "Course he'll win."

"Verily," the stranger said, and clapped them both on their backs. "You've seen the scroll—how can I fail?"

Then they watched him mount his old nag of a horse and ascend the peak. They were still watching him an hour later. It was a tall peak.

"Now here's what I think," said the butcher, as if taking up a ball to resume a familiar game of catch. "If we were a little more honest abou' the *size* o' the dragon—"

"Then he never would have agreed to go up there," the baker finished.

"Maybe. Maybe. Or just maybe he'd be better prepared when he did go. I don't think they told Hercules he was after the three-headed lapdog o' Dingle Bay, is what I'm sayin'."

They heard a noise then and looked up, but it was only one of the vultures. They couldn't see the stranger anymore. Just now he'd probably be finding his way down the slope of a huge black bowl at the top of the mountain, filled with ashes and dead wood. Or so they were told—neither man had ever seen it for himself.

"Won't be long now," the butcher murmured.

"I think Declan Sage knows what he's doin'," said the baker.

"I suppose," the butcher relented.

And because neither of them said anything at all for a while, he added, "I didn't get his name, did you?"

Then a bit of color caught their eye, and they raised their heads to see a streak of blue flame shoot off the mountain like an exclamation point.

The butcher winced. "Should I really have been able to hear him scream from here?"

In the Village of Reek, Declan Sage carefully rolled the Scroll of Prophecy halfway, then paused. He touched a finger to the paint at the Chosen One's hair and clothes, but it was dry, of course it was dry. It had probably been dry for hours now. He rolled it the rest of the way up, made as if to take the scroll back to his study . . . then reconsidered and threw the whole thing in the trash. The chances of another stranger with the same hair and clothes happening by were pretty slim, after all, and he needed the space.

CHAPTER 1

In Pretannica, morning was when you woke up.

In the blue twilight there were little mornings stirring at every moment, all over the magical land. When the farmer rose to feed his pigs it was morning, and morning again when the apple man wheeled his cart into the square. It was morning for the tower guard when he roused some twelve hours later for the start of his watch; later still when the town drunkard woke to consider where his trousers had gone—and just why he was clutching this weather vane—only to be chased down from the rooftop by the tower guard, through the town square and consequently the apple cart, and to the edge of town, where he rested in a mud bank nestled between warm pigs and was found by the farmer six hours later.

It was always twilight in Pretannica. Morning was what you made it.

Scott couldn't have told you if his morning resembled the farmer's, or apple man's, or guard's or drunkard's. He was on his own time, driving himself to exhaustion as he struggled to stay a step ahead of the trooping fairies that were tracking him.

Even Mick was on his own time, Scott noted once more as he awoke and found the leprechaun to be gone. Mick couldn't sleep much with all the glamour in the air, or didn't need to. He was probably off searching for breakfast or firewood.

Scott had gone and done something stupid. He'd suggested to Titania, High Queen of the Fay, that maybe she didn't have to conquer the human race after all. That maybe there was a way she could lead the fairies to Earth and then . . . just let the humans bask in their magic. Worship their weird celebrity; give them reality shows to star in and network dance competitions to judge. He had put it better when he'd pleaded his case at court. But Titania had thrown Mick and him in a prison cell all the same.

Scott had gotten through to Titania's favorite changeling, though. He'd done that much. Dhanu had set them free and helped them escape before they split up. Now the elves were likely hunting him, too.

Dhanu probably hadn't spent the last six hours snoring in a bramble patch, though. Scott sniffed himself, winced inwardly, and shuffled down to the stream to wash.

On the bank of the stream he startled some kind of long-necked, long-legged wading bird, which spread its wide wings and honked at him.

"Sorry," Scott answered, and put his hands up in a don't-shoot kind of gesture that probably didn't mean the same thing in the animal kingdom. The bird honked a second time, and its wings folded up like a road map, and its neck retracted and its legs ratcheted up into its belly, and then it improbably folded up a couple more times and disappeared into thin air.

Scott stared, fuddled. "All right." He sighed, and undressed.

There were blackberry stains on his clothes, and the general stains of a life badly lived, and most of these would not come out. "Doesn't matter," Scott muttered to himself, remembering something his mother used to say: "It's not like I'm gonna be meeting the queen." Except there was a better-than-average chance that he *was* going to be meeting the queen. He tried to put it out of his mind and scrubbed himself as well as possible in the brisk water.

"Tell me when you're done," said someone, and Scott flinched, slipped on the slick river stones, and did his best to hide himself in the shallow creek.

"Wh . . . what? Who are you?"

"Tsk. You've already forgotten. Seems to me that if you kill someone, the classy thing to do is remember him."

Scott squinted in the direction of the voice, but there was nothing but reeds, trees, a bit of mist hanging over a rock. Mist, or gnats, or . . .

"Is that you?" Scott asked the mist. It was just slightly person shaped. More and more so, the longer he stared at it.

"Seeing as I'm facing the forest, champ, I can't really tell what you're looking at. You want me to turn around?"

Scott scrambled for his sopping clothes and pulled them on. "You're facing away from me," Scott said, more to himself than to the mist. Knowing this made it easier to make out the back of a head, a neck, a skinny body dressed in a phantom T-shirt and pants.

"Seemed like the decent thing to do," said the mist. "I would have just closed my eyes, but when you're a ghost it turns out you can see through your own eyelids."

"A ghost . . . ," said Scott. "H—Haskoll?"

"He remembers!" The ghost of Haskoll turned around. "Hey, lookin' sharp, big guy. Never let anyone tell you ya can't pull off this whole wet 'n' filthy look. I think it's brave."

"Haskoll," Scott whispered. "Haskoll's a ghost." Then, louder: "Have you been following us around all this time?"

Haskoll sniffed. "Not *all* this time. I stayed with my body awhile. Just until somebody found it. All these

airline investigators came out to deal with the wreckage."

Last November Haskoll had been crushed by a piece of falling airplane. While trying to kill Scott, as it happened, so Scott had been okay with the whole episode, because he'd assumed he would never have to talk to Haskoll about it.

He coughed and nodded at the ghost. "Of course. It was . . . probably hard to leave your body. Right? It was all you'd ever known, and—"

"Nah. I just wanted to see their faces when they cleared away the engine and found a whole guy under there. Nearly a whole guy."

"Oh."

"Listen to you—'It was all you'd ever known.' You should have a daytime talk show."

Scott climbed the rest of the way out of the creek. Could a ghost hurt him? Maybe Haskoll's ghost was here for revenge.

"Then after they cleared the airplane off me, I spied on ladies for a while, and then I thought, 'I wonder what that nice kid who murdered me has gotten up to,' and I tracked you down. With my ghost powers."

"*I* murdered *you*?" Scott blustered. "Are you kidding? Harvey magicked a piece of airplane out of the sky because *you* were about to shoot *me*." Technically, the rabbit-man Harvey had probably done this more from fear of getting captured than out of any regard for Scott, but whatever. *Plus, you deserved what you got,* Scott wanted to say. *You were working for Goodco.* And yes, sure, Scott's *mom* worked for Goodco too, but his mom didn't know it was a nefarious organization run by a wicked fairy queen who wanted to conquer the earth for her people. Haskoll had known *exactly* who he was working for.

Ghost Haskoll shrugged his insubstantial shoulders. "Somebody was gonna shoot someone with somewhat; that's all ancient history. So, what did I miss?"

"Miss?"

"I mean, what's been going on since I died?"

"Oh. Um. Well, we all escaped from Goodco," said Scott. "Me and Mick and Harvey and Erno and Emily and Biggs. Oh, and my dad and sister. And this guy Merle."

"I don't like stories with too many characters."

"Then the Lady of the Lake, Nimue, she tried to put a spell on us. I whacked her with a pole."

"Rude."

"One of my sister's toys ended up being this enchanted pixie prince named Fi. So he came with us too, on the run, and I sent my mom a year into the future to protect her. We went on a cruise. I ate a magic fish and knew everything in the world, but then I forgot it."

"Tough break."

"And . . . um . . . we found a way to get to Pretannica,

because we learned that Nimue was keeping the Queen of England prisoner here. Because the queen can knight people, and only knights can kill dragons, and Nimue wants to bring this huge pink dragon named Saxbriton to Earth to protect her while she turns all the Goodco customers into zombies and opens a huge door between Earth and Pretannica. And I visited the High Queen of the fairies and tried to convince her not to invade Earth, but. Well, that didn't work out too good. But my dad and Merle rescued Queen Elizabeth, apparently, except now we're all trapped here and can't get home."

"Look at you!" said Haskoll. "Busy little guy. No more murders, though?"

"I'm not a murderer!"

"I was just a special case, huh? I guess I should be flattered."

"If . . . if you died you have no one to blame but yourself. It was you—"

Haskoll made a yak-yak-yak gesture with his ghostly hand. "Whatever. You gotta let this thing go—I'm not here to play the blame game. Hey! Maybe I'm here to play the name game!"

"The what?"

Ghost Haskoll leaped to his feet. "Haskoll Haskoll bo baskoll banana fanana fo faskoll! Mee mi mo maskoll!" he shouted. "I Iaskoll!"

"Can we maybe—" Scott interjected.

"Let's do Harvey! Harvey Harvey bo barvey banana fanana fo farvey! Mee mi mo marvey! Harvey! Let's do the kid who murdered me! Scott Scott bo bott! Banana fanana fo fott—"

Just then Mick pushed through the reeds and stopped at the water's edge.

"Let's do Mick! Mick Mick bo bick—"

"There yeh are," Mick told Scott. "When I got back t' camp an' found yeh gone, I worried."

"Sorry," said Scott. "Um." Mick hadn't appeared to notice Haskoll at all, despite the ghost singing and doing the running man right behind him.

"We should get goin'," said Mick.

"Yeah. Yeah. So . . . ," said Scott as he pulled his boots on. "Can the Fay usually see ghosts?"

Mick chuckled. "Ghosts? There's no such thing, lad."

"Says the leprechaun," said Haskoll. Scott watched him over his shoulder as he and Mick made their way back to camp.

"Take care, buddy!" Haskoll added. "See you again soon!"

CHAPTER 2

The young pixie prince named Fee clutched the sill of
the backseat window, watching the world pass and pivot
around them.

"We are looking for . . . what was it, brother?" he asked.
"A riff?"

"A rift," said Fi. "A door. A way to make the Crossing."

The others, Fo and Denzil and tiny Polly, struggled
with their dignity as they tumbled around the backseat of
the taxicab. The pooka Harvey was a spirited driver, and
he made each turn as though he'd only thought of it at
the last possible second. The mechanical owl, Archimedes, clutched a headrest and swayed in perfect gyroscopic
counterbalance to everything Harvey did.

"And this Crossing will take us back to our own
world?" asked Fee.

"Aye, little brother. And we will save Scott and Mick

from the elves, and show them the doors on Fray's island that can take them home."

"And see Morenwyn again, and convince her to join us," added Fee.

Fi looked out the window. "Perhaps."

With a shriek, the cab bucked and came to a stop. Polly and the three princes tumbled down onto the floor mats.

"It'th thomewhere around here," Harvey told them. "You know *I* can't thee it."

"I'll be able to," said Polly. "Can you open the door?"

"Hold, Polly," said Fi. "We should take care how we exit the taxi wagon. Goodco and the Freemen may well have this rift guarded."

"No one around but thome human on the nextht block," Harvey told them.

Denzil consulted the map on Merle's watch. "The rift we sought is on a large city circus. This is not that rift."

"Yeah," Harvey agreed with a wave. "I took you thome-place elthe—to a quieter part of town. There'th a real nice rift here, leadth to the bank of a little pool."

"How big is it?" asked Polly.

"Big enough for . . . like a thmall cat."

"Or a rabbit?" said Fi. "How do you know of this rift, exactly?"

Harvey shrugged. "You know, I hear thingth. Big earsth an' all. You want me to drive you to the other rift?

I'll drive you to the other rift."

"This is good," said Polly. "Right? Quieter, like you said."

Fi gave Harvey a last look, then he and Polly and the other three princes dropped out of the cab and down to the quiet street. The same person still stood alone on the next block. They crept around the rear tire and peered at this person, standing stiffly under a distant streetlamp.

"You think that's where the Crossing is?" Polly asked Fi.

"I expect so."

"And the Crossing's guarded."

"Indeed it is."

Polly squinted. "That's a crossing guard."

The figure under the streetlight was a stout, elderly Pakistani woman wearing a safety-yellow cap and rain slicker striped with reflective strips. She held a tall pole that was like a wizard's staff, if you happened to believe that wizards' staffs were topped with red-and-yellow stop signs, which Polly didn't.

"What do you think, brother?" Denzil whispered to Fi. "Troll?"

"It's not a troll," said Polly. "It's an old lady who helps kids cross the street. Look—she's standing on a crosswalk and everything."

"I *was* thinking troll," Fi confided, "as it is guarding a

bridge, so to speak. But trolls are no shape-shifters."

"Probably just an old lady, then," said Polly.

Harvey arched his neck out the window. "You gonna be okay?" he asked Polly. "I got thingth to do."

Polly looked down at the crossing guard and back up at the pooka.

"I guess so." She beamed him a smile. "Well...thanks."

If Harvey didn't answer right away, it was only because he'd never been thanked for anything before. He wasn't sure what one did in situations like this. Finally he nodded, and Polly and the pixies helped one another up the curb.

"Could it be an ogre?" asked Fo as they crept down the block.

"Not an ogre," said Polly. "Lady."

"Possibly an ogre," Fi admitted. "Or an ogress? I've never heard tell of such a thing, but 'the twilight's liminal light doth veil a thousand fairy faces,' as they say."

"No one says that," Polly told them. "It's not an ogress. In this world there are these people called crossing guards, see, and they help kids get to school."

"And is school in session now?" Fee asked.

You could tell he wasn't being snarky about it—he honestly didn't know. But it *was* the middle of the night. Polly reluctantly admitted that there was really no reason for the woman to be here. Then she saw the rift.

"It's there," she whispered, straining to see the shimmery flicker of it. "Right between the woman's feet. It's really small."

Funny, calling something small when it was easily a whole head taller than she was. Maybe now she should call everything medium or large, she thought, the way they do in fast-food restaurants.

"So . . . ," said Polly. "Maybe we're so small we can just sneak right through her feet?"

Fo harumphed. "A pixie does not *sneak*. A pixie announces himself to his foe, like a gentleman."

"Does he die like a gentleman too?" asked Polly. "Like when his foe steps on him?"

A cat meowed nearby, and they all tensed. Several seconds passed without incident, so they continued up the block. They'd be at the intersection soon.

"The great hero Cornwallace never sneaked," said Fee. "He looked each villain in the eye before thrashing him."

"My brother forgets the song of Cornwallace and the honeycomb treasure," Denzil whispered. "He dressed like a bee."

Fee shook his head. "I don't accept the songs as part of official canon. A magic everlasting honeycomb? If it's so everlasting, how come I've never seen it?"

"Cornwallace also used trickery during his adventure in the palace of the mole king."

"He was facing a *ronopolisk*. Unarmed!"

"Perhaps we can at least agree, then, that a pixie sneaks when he hasn't any other option."

"Well," said Polly. "*I'm* not a pixie. Are you gonna get grossed out if I start sneaking right in front of you?"

Fi coughed. "May I propose that we settle this another time?" he said. "As the troll has been eyeing us these past two minutes, I sense the point is moot."

They stopped and fixed their eyes on the crossing guard. She was leaning on her stop sign, watching them. She waved.

Polly and the pixies waited for a car to pass, then hopped down the curb.

"This is going really good so far," said Polly. "They're probably gonna write a song about us, too."

"Fee, Fi, Fo, Fum!" said the crossing guard with a rubbery grin.

"It's Denzil, actually," said Denzil.

"And Polly."

"That's not as funny," the woman said. "I was gonna say, 'I smell the blood of some pixie men,' but . . . forget it, it's ruined now."

"You were expecting us," said Fi, and his hand went to the sword at his side. His brothers reached for their belts too, out of habit, but they hadn't any weapons.

"Was it supposed to be a secret?" said the guard. "Your

little jailbreak? With its chemical spill and alarms and man-eating manticore? You lot are about as subtle as a turd." Her grin quivered. There was something flabby about the way it hung on her face. "I weren't expecting a tiny girl, I'll give you that."

"I drank potions at the Goodco labs!" said Polly. She'd decided that "potions" sounded less irresponsible than "chemicals."

"You don't say," said the guard.

"I do say. Because I realized: how could they get the queen across the Crossing unless they made her really small? Right? 'Cause Goodco only knows about really small rifts like the one between your feet. So I took chemicals until I found the right ones to shrink me and I accidentally got really tiny wings too but I like them even though they aren't good for anything," she finished. She thought she'd been pretty clever back at Goodco and felt that she wasn't getting enough credit for it.

The crossing guard wasn't impressed, anyway. She laughed with an unpleasant huff that waggled the slack corners of her mouth.

"Oh. Oh, gross," said Polly. "Ew ew ew that's just a costume, isn't it? Please say it's not real old-lady skin."

"You like?" The troll raised her arms. Where the skin showed, she looked dark and dimpled as an overstuffed chair. "Coupla goblins made it for me. Not really my size, but it keeps the sun off."

"There's *no way* that fools anyone during the day," said Polly. "The kids must be terrified of you."

The troll stepped forward, and shadows pooled in the pits and sockets of her face. "They *are* terrified of me," she said, and you could hear the giddiness in her voice. "But they don't know why. They whisper stories to one another—I hear them, I have very good ears. I'm a witch, or a serial killer. I eat children and keep a cellar full of bones. And it's all true. Children always know. Don't you, love?"

"Step aside and let us use the rift," announced Fi. "And though you be a dreadful thing, you will not be harmed."

"Heh. Cute."

"Charge, my brothers!"

The pixies surged forward. Polly started. "What? We're just rushing the troll? Hoo . . . okay." She screamed her high-pitched little-girl scream and ran forward with the rest.

The pixie brothers reached the troll as a group but scattered as her foot came down in the middle of them.

"Polly! Where is the rift?"

"Here! Here!"

"Stand in it and make ready! We will distract the brute!"

"I can hear you, you know," said the troll.

Fee, Fo, and Denzil could only strike at the monster with their fists. And though pixies were strong for their size, the troll was oblivious. Denzil managed by leaps and bounds to scale his way to her shoulders, but when he struck her chin she shook like a wet dog and sent him sailing into a hedge.

"Brother! The rift does not work! Polly remains!"

"I have to wait for something on the other side!" said Polly.

The troll cackled and kicked. Fo caught the edge of her sneaker and tumbled into the street. Soon this same sneaker appeared above Polly, blotting out the light of the streetlamp, and she had no choice but to run or be squashed. Fi appeared at her side and slashed at the troll's heel with his sword. He cut through both sock and goblin skin to reveal something shaggy and foul underneath.

"Ow! Little pest."

"Brothers! We must withdraw!"

At this, Fi continued to prod and slash at the troll's feet while the other three pixies arranged their fingers in their mouths and whistled.

Polly peeked out from under the hedge. "What are they doing?" she asked.

"Whimpering like little babies," answered the troll.

"Calling to the nightingales, in the manner of a lost

fledgling," corrected Fi, and he stabbed through the toe of her sneaker.

"OW!"

And before long a small flock of confused mother nightingales alighted on the hedgerow. One even swooped close to the troll and beat her wings in her face.

Each of the brothers rushed now to grab at a tail or a tuft of feathers or a leg. The birds, startled, took to the air. Prince Fi curled his arm around Polly's waist and managed to catch hold of a single talon as the last nightingale flew away.

"EEEEEEEEEEEEEEE!" screamed Polly as they rose, air whooshing all around, the dizzy city streets dropping out from under them.

Through whistling and cajoling, the brothers managed to keep the birds together, and they all reconvened in a cherry tree three houses away. Polly and the brothers dropped free and clutched at branches as the angry nightingales flapped and snapped at them.

Fee stood recklessly upright on a swaying cherry branch as the birds moved away. "We will redouble our efforts and attack again before the troll woman has a chance to recover," he said.

"Recover from what, exactly?" said Denzil.

"Maybe we should just try another rift," said Polly. "That troll's probably calling Goodco right now, an' there'll be a thousand army men here soon."

Fi looked thoughtful. "I doubt that. She's shown quite handily that she doesn't need the help, and trolls are solitary creatures."

Polly shinnied up the branch toward him. "What else do you know about trolls?"

"Hmm. That they're meant to be slow-witted, but this one seems plenty canny."

"And that they're afraid of thunder, supposedly," said Fo.

"And that sunlight will turn them to stone," added Denzil.

"I've never heard that," said Fee.

"It's a lesson from our oldest stories, written and told when our world had a sun, and seasons. But she's already told us her skin suit protects her."

Polly frowned. "Does it have to be sunlight, or any light?"

"Sunlight. There is in the sun's rays some special property fearsome to trolls."

Polly bounced on her branch, and the others grasped at twigs to keep from falling. "I know this!" she said. "My mom says it *constantly*. The sun has lots of UV light! Ultraviolet. It's not so good for people, either—that's why she's always smearing me with sunscreen."

"Well," said Fee. "This is all well and good if we want to skulk like magpies in this tree all night, waiting for the sun. Unless you can make it shine at night? And there's still the troll's suit to consider."

Polly thought. Mom was a scientist and was always starting sentences with "Here's something interesting" or "Have you ever wondered?" Polly mostly just pretended to listen while she thought about soccer or her birthday. And now she wished Mom were here with her, for only the seven hundredth time this week.

"I . . . I bet I could get us a UV light . . . ," she began. "The birds might know what I'm thinking of, if they're still willing to help us. Could you ask if any of them know a good place for dead bugs around here?"

The troll (whose name was Underfoot; and whose True Name was Mó-Andlit; and who, in her own private poetry, referred to herself as Gladiola) thought she may as well call it in to Goodco, now. Now that half an hour had passed since the pixies fled, now that it seemed clear they wouldn't be trying again tonight. She'd tell Goodco and their idiot Freemen that the little smurfs had only *just* left, of course. Hurry and you might still catch them, she'd say.

She'd just fished her phone from the pocket of her rain slicker when a nightingale swooped low, right in front of her face, and perched atop the hedge on the troll's corner. The bird (who, if he'd had a name, would have called himself Biggest and Loudest, like all other male nightingales) then commenced to twitter and shriek and make its ray-gun noises at the troll as lustily as it could.

"Shoo," the troll told it, frowning her Pakistaniwoman face. She wished she could show the bird her *real* face—that would shut it up. She scanned the gutter for something to throw and missed the second nightingale dropping a tiny prince on her rounded back. But she felt the pixie's sword when it bit into her backbone.

"YEARGH!" the troll bellowed as she twisted and whipped her arms about. "Back for more, blueberry?"

Fi's weapon, the marginally enchanted sword known as Carpet Nail, was stuck fast in the monster's back. Fi hung two-handed from its hilt. But he swung himself into a high backflip, landed feetfirst on the crossing guard, and catapulted himself into another flip to avoid the swipe of the troll's lacquered nails.

Finally he was falling, and on his way down Fi once again grabbed the hilt of his sword and rode it down the troll's back as it sliced a ragged line through both slicker and goblin skin.

"AAH!" said the troll. "Stupid! You're gonna ruin it!"

She shook herself again, dislodging Carpet Nail and sending Fi sprawling into the street and beneath the wheel of an oncoming car, which the pixie prince only narrowly avoided. Meanwhile the tear in the troll's suit spread like a split seam.

"No! No!"

With the bang of a burst balloon, both skin and clothes flew off in tatters, and the troll was revealed as the shaggy giantess she really was.

Now easily twice as large as she'd been just a moment before, she windmilled her ape arms and roared. Nearly every inch of her was covered in a patchwork of coarse and silken hair, into which were tangled and braided a collection of chicken bones, twigs, dried mushrooms and turnips, rutabagas, teeth. Her black mane coursed with mice. Beady eyes flashed above her big butternut nose.

Fi circled around her and she followed his path, turning her back to the street.

"You think you're clever?" she asked him. "You're STUPID STUPID STUPID! It won't be dawn for HOURS! All I have to do is call for backup!"

Fi crouched near the hedge. "With what phone, fair lady?" he asked her.

She'd crushed her phone. She squinted now at the glittering mess of it.

"RAAA!" she said, and Fi leaped as she tore the entire hedge out by the roots. "Doesn't matter! I'll get the Freemen here even if I have to set fire to this whole neighborhood! YEEEEEAAH! WHAT?"

In her fury she'd missed three more pixies (and one

pixie-sized girl) rushing across the street with a boxy object on their shoulders between them, like pallbearers late to a funeral. But this boxy thing was more like a cage than a coffin, and it glowed with purple light.

"BUG ZAPPERRR!" Polly called as they rammed the troll's heel with it. It wasn't all that much UV light, not really, but half her ankle scabbed over with a stony crust. The troll lurched and kicked the black cage out of the hands of Polly and the pixies, and it skidded down the street.

They started after it. "I thought we all agreed we were gonna yell 'bug zapper' when we hit her," Polly complained to the brothers. "Like for a battle cry."

"*You* agreed," said Fee.

"When the moment came, I just wasn't feeling it," said Denzil.

The troll pivoted to follow them, and her petrified heel crackled and crumbled. Fi raced forward and drove his sword into the sole of her good foot, and the troll woman timbered like a tree. The asphalt trembled.

"Whuh," she moaned, stunned.

The solar panels atop the bug zapper were cracked. But the cage had protected the UV bulb, which still glowed like purple neon. The pixie brothers hefted their weapon again and heaved it against the troll's eyes. The howl that followed made dogs bark, milk sour, car alarms wail all over the north of London. She was still howling seconds later when she got to her ruined feet, stumbled blindly into the road, and was hit by a newspaper truck.

"Oof. Is she okay?" asked Polly.

"She sleeps. Quickly, to the rift," said Fi. "She won't be out for long."

Despite his earlier impatience, Harvey had not yet moved. Instead he'd watched the whole business with the troll in his rearview mirror as Merlin's owl perched beside him, still as a statue.

"Archimedeeth," said the pooka.

The bird didn't respond.

"Arc-i-*mee*-deesthh," Harvey repeated, wrestling with his lisp. "Arc-i-me . . ." He sighed. "Archie."

The owl's head swiveled to face him.

"The Utth kids. Erno and Emily," Harvey told it. "Can you find them?"

CHAPTER 3

The London Zoo was quiet at night. It was so quiet that every little noise carried, and occasionally some shrill howl or guttural growl reached Erno's and Emily's ears and lit sparks in the oldest parts of their brains—the caveman parts that implored them to run, climb the nearest tree, escape danger. But they were already in a tree, so that was okay.

Biggs had gotten them up into the tree, of course, along with Erno's suitcase and the few things of Emily's that they'd managed to throw into a shopping bag before fleeing the row house they'd been living in. Now they realized that they really should have concentrated on gathering Biggs's things, since he was the one with the money and credit cards. The poor big man shivered in his pajamas, cradling the unicat in his arms. Erno was reminded of that sign-language gorilla with the pet kitten.

Emily fiddled with her headgear. "What time is it?" she asked, and the question made Erno sad. She couldn't check the time herself because she was currently clinging to a tree limb with her eyes closed—she wasn't any more fond of heights now than she had been the last time they'd been forced up a tree. But that wasn't what bothered Erno.

He could still remember the day, when they were four, when Emily asked why so many people wore watches.

Erno hadn't paused to consider why she was asking. When you're four you're used to fielding a lot of questions, mostly from adults who already knew the answers—they just wanted to see if *you* did. So, without looking up from his Legos, Erno had answered, "To tell the time."

"But why don't they already *know* the time?"

Now Erno paused. He didn't understand a question like this one. "I dunno."

"*You* know the time, don't you?" asked Emily. "It's twelve thirty-four."

Erno got up and walked into the dining room to check the big cuckoo clock. It took him some time to remember what the hands meant, and by the time he'd figured it out it was technically 12:35, but still.

He rejoined Emily in the living room. "How'd you know that?" he'd asked, even though he'd begun to suspect that this and so many other questions about Emily had the same answer.

"I look at the clock in my brain," she said. "Don't you have a brain clock that counts the seconds?"

Erno gave this some thought. "Yes," he lied. It was the first such lie, the first of many.

Now, in a tree in the London Zoo, Erno understood that Emily had lost her brain clock. Or worse, she'd made the choice to stop counting.

"It's three fifteen," he said. By four a.m. they needed to be at the subway entrance at Oxford Circus, because they'd left instructions for Polly and Fi to meet them there. Polly, Fi, or anyone else they trusted who might have happened to ask the mechanical owl Archimedes how to find them. Just to regroup. Just to figure out what their next move ought to be. If no one showed by five, they'd try back every two hours until someone did.

None of them had gotten any sleep.

"Maybe we should get going, then," Emily said. "We might have to walk the whole way."

Biggs got them down from the tree, shivering all the while. There was literally no item of Erno's or Emily's clothing that would have done him a bit of good. He couldn't even get one of Erno's socks over the flippers he called feet.

As they walked back past the bearded pig exhibit to the outer wall of the zoo, Erno told Biggs, "If I see a big blanket or a . . . car cover or *something*, I'm going to steal it for you."

"St-stealing's wrong," Biggs chattered.

"So is letting a person freeze to death."

"'S okay," the big man said. "Be w-warmer soon."

"Soon as in when the sun comes up?" said Emily. "Or soon meaning in a few days when all your body hair's grown back and you look like Sasquatch?"

Erno hadn't planned to mention this himself, but it was true that Biggs hadn't shaved for more than a day now, and nearly every square inch of his visible skin had a gray, sandpapery look to it. Anyway, Biggs didn't answer her. He held his tongue as he gathered up the kids and their bags and jumped from the trash can to the signpost and then over the zoo wall.

Emily hauled her own bag and Erno pulled his own suitcase through the park. They were alone here.

"What time is it now?" asked Emily.

"Three nineteen."

"I did the right thing," Emily said. It wasn't exactly a question, but if it went without saying, then she wouldn't be saying it, Erno thought. "I told Nimue about the row house. I didn't mean to, but she sneaked into my dreams again. I had to close that rift in the basement while I still could," she added. "Before Nimue got it, before she took control of my mind again."

Erno nodded his head. "Yeah . . . ," he said. "I guess it's gonna be hard for Scott and John and everybody to get home now."

"They'll figure it out. Scott's *very* smart. They'll go visit Fi's pixie witch—she has rifts back to Earth. Or they'll get back later, when Nimue opens the big rift to bring her people through." Emily's tone was calm, self-assured. But after each calmly self-assured statement she glanced at Erno out of the corner of her eye.

"Can't really see the elves letting them use their big rift," Erno said with a kind of vocal shrug, like he didn't feel too strongly either way about it. Like he expected to be wrong, like he always expected to be wrong.

"Why not? Why would they stop them? I don't think they'd stop them."

"You're probably right."

"I know I'm right. I had to do what I did, collapsing the rift in the basement. It was the right thing, it was necessary."

They walked for a minute in silence. Then Biggs, who had been carrying the unicat and quietly rubbing the circulation back into his arms, spoke.

"Forgive you," he said.

So Emily broke into tears.

It was just Biggs's way of speaking, but it came out like he was both offering forgiveness and maybe commanding

Emily to forgive herself. He scooped her up, and she leaned into his chest.

They were exiting the park now, stepping through city streets. They saw a few people—mostly piles of laundry that turned out to be men curled up in doorways. A boxy truck was stopped at the corner, back door raised, insides lit and filled with newspapers. A man heaved a stack of these papers onto the curb. Then the man turned away, and Erno grabbed one as they passed.

Below the fold there was a headline: SEARCH FOR DWIGHT CONTINUES AS GOODCO QUESTIONED.

Law enforcement continues to investigate the disappearance of film and pop superstar Reggie Dwight after his controversial "summit" with Queen Elizabeth at the British Museum in March. Dwight assaulted Elizabeth II in front of press and onlookers in a self-proclaimed attempt to expose the queen as an impostor.

The incident was complicated by the alleged appearance of a fire-breathing bird and a tiny swordsman. Both bird and swordsman appeared to be allied with Dwight and may have contributed to his escape from the museum. The morning was later marked by eyewitness accounts of a giant in adjacent Russell

Square. The so-called giant's body was allegedly recovered by individuals claiming to be police officers. An official statement from the City of London police denies any knowledge of the giant.

An unconfirmed email message from Reggie Dwight sought to shed light on the actor/singer's behavior, claiming that the queen has at an unspecified point in the past been replaced by a look-alike under the guidance of the Goodco Cereal Company, makers of such breakfast staples as Honey Frosted Snox and Puftees. The email contained a list of grievances against Goodco, including accusations of unlawful human experimentation and of mind control through the use of an unauthorized chemical additive in Peanut Butter Clobbers. Goodco has marketed Clobbers and other cereals with language suggesting that it increases intelligence via a formula called Intellijuice. An official statement from Goodco calls Intellijuice a "fictional ingredient" on par with Cud cereal's Chocanilla, Puftees cereal's Crispity Purplegrape, or Pooberries (from the short-lived Disgustees, which was found by the U.K. Food Standards Agency to contain no berries and only trace amounts of animal waste). "Peanut Butter Clobbers increases intelligence only in the sense that any healthy, delicious breakfast contributes to a person's ability to concentrate and capacity to learn," the statement concluded.

The Official Reggie Dwight Fan Club has called for a boycott of all Goodco products, including noncereal products such as Velveteen Cheese Loaf and Kobold Snack Biscuits, and public opinion polls show that a significant minority of consumers are similarly avoiding the Goodco brand. Independent agencies, meanwhile, have issued preliminary reports stating that consuming Peanut Butter Clobbers does raise IQ scores, but they caution that more research is needed.

In spite of these competing and contradictory claims, sales of Peanut Butter Clobbers have outpaced all other breakfast cereals, prompting Goodco to release a limited-edition variety called OOPS! Just Sugar, which contains only the strawberry-flavored Intellijuice pieces.

"Well," Erno muttered, "at least *some* people are listening to us."

He didn't realize how close they were to the meeting place. He'd been paying more attention to the paper, and he didn't really know London, after all. There were more people on the streets now, though; more people to stare nakedly at Biggs as he passed in his bare feet and pajamas, clutching a tiny girl in one arm like he might at any moment start climbing buildings and swatting at airplanes. The unicat rested in Emily's shopping bag.

It was Biggs who first noticed the rabbit-man.

"Harvey," he said.

It was *only* Harvey, it seemed, waiting by one of the entrances to the Underground. He had the owl Archimedes on his shoulder and Merle's watch on his wrist, but no pixie, no Polly. As far as they could tell, anyway—it would be hard to see Fi from here. Harvey gave a little half-wave. Londoners passed him from time to time but didn't pay him any notice. These people wouldn't see Harvey until the rabbit-man wanted to be seen.

A sign on the subway entrance said that this station was closed for servicing. Emily frowned at it, and at Harvey.

"I thought Polly and Fi would be with you," she said.

"Good to thee you too," said Harvey. "Clever of you to ethcape the row houthe."

"Polly and Fi must have gone off on their own, then," said Emily. "If you have the owl, then there's no way for them to know where to meet us. We need to send Archie back up to St. George's Avenue to wait for them."

"Clever of you to collapthe the rift, too," said Harvey. "You lot are like mothquitoeth—taking a little blood here, a little there. Pethtering Nimue but never doing her any real harm. Mothquitoeth."

Biggs sniffed the air.

"Mosquitoes carry malaria," said Erno. "And West Nile virus. Maybe we're giving her West Nile virus."

"Run," said Emily.

"What?" Erno said as he turned to her. She looked wild, terror stricken, a mouse caught in a trap. He didn't realize what a trapped mouse he was too, until he heard the dull thuds of a dozen tranquilizer darts hitting Biggs at once. Erno dropped to the sidewalk and scanned the rooftops—they were crawling with snipers.

Biggs was still on his feet, but staggering, more concerned with setting Emily down safely than fleeing or defending himself. He whined deep down in his throat, like a dog.

A battery of black-and-pink-clad men quickstepped up the subway stairs now and stood behind Harvey. Freemen, loyal members of the secret society at the heart of Goodco. They all had Tasers at the ready.

"They found me outthide the Goodco plant north of London," Harvey said, "while Polly and Fi were inthide. They offered me a chanthe to . . . renew my contract with the company. I uthed to deliver Milk-Theven for them, you thee—I delivered a lot of thingth, back and forth acroth the smaller riftth, in the form of a rabbit. I was a hoppy little bunny for Team Nimue."

"You were never on their team," Emily said quietly, breathily. "Or ours. You've always been for yourself and yourself only."

"Exthactly. And it wath that attitude that got me locked up and my glamour milked back in the thixthties. But I've theen the error of my wayth. Me an' Goodco have agreed to let bygonth be bygonth."

"So what happened to Polly and Fi?" growled Erno. "Did you turn them in, too?"

Harvey glanced at the Freemen. "You know, I wath thuppothed to, but they gave me the thlip. They were thmarter than you three, I gueth."

Biggs was on the ground now, breathing shallowly. His eyelids fluttered as Emily cradled his head.

"Honethtly, look at you," said Harvey. "All of you. You're a meth. You can barely keep from defeating your-thelveth. How're you gonna beat Nimue?"

Erno clenched his fists—knowing it would be ridiculous to try to fight off twelve Freemen; seriously considering it anyway. "You're never gonna get your glamour back, you know," he said. "Mick says you have to be good. Or . . . honorable, at least. You'll lose it all and never get it back."

Harvey blew a raspberry. "That'th Mick'th fairy tale, not mine. The univerth don't care what we do."

"Bull," Emily whispered. "You only *wish* you didn't believe it."

Harvey might have flinched, then. "What?"

"You *wish* you didn't believe in honor. But you do. You came back to help Mick at the Freemen's Temple in Goodborough. You *let* Polly escape, because you like her more than the rest of us. You wish you were half as good as Mick, but you're too big a coward for that. You're a bunny rabbit, Harvey, a timid little forest creature. You're *prey*, and you'll always be prey."

Harvey just glared. Then he huffed. "*I'm* prey? I'm not the one about to be fitted for a cage."

"Course not," Emily told him. "Why would they bother? It took them fifty years, but Goodco finally learned they don't *need* to cage you. You're tame."

Harvey trembled. "Shut *up*. Shut your ugly mouth. Will thomeone pleathe shut her up?" he spat, before the Freemen circled around to collect their prisoners.

CHAPTER 4

"What's he look like?" Mick asked Scott. "I can't see."

Scott squinted down the cobblestone road from the safety of the bushes. A traveler approached. "Like, middle-aged, I guess," Scott whispered. "Riding a donkey. I'm pretty sure he's human, and maybe blind?"

"Why blind?"

"'Cause he has a blindfold on."

"If he were blind, why would he need a blindfold?"

"If he weren't blind, why would he want a blindfold? I don't know, maybe he has really gross eyes?"

"Well, I say we stop 'im," said Mick. "Maybe he'll wanna trade some food for all this gold I keep findin'."

Scott stepped out into the road, and the donkey immediately brayed. The blindfolded man fumbled with a crossbow that was slung over his shoulders. "Um, sorry," Scott said. "Hi. I didn't mean to scare you, I just wondered if you had any food I could buy."

"You sound like just a boy," the man said, and he reached for his blindfold. Then he seemed to think better of this, and left it where it was. "Or a young lady."

"Boy."

"Are you alone, boy?"

"More or less."

"For heaven's sake, lad, run home to your mother! The ronopolisk is loose!"

Scott frowned. He didn't know what that was. He considered himself kind of an expert on fantasy monsters and still resented it whenever anyone tried to tell him something he hadn't already heard of. He turned to where Mick watched through the bushes and mouthed "Ronopolisk?" but the leprechaun just shrugged.

"Well . . . thanks. I'll keep an eye out. So do you want to sell any food?"

"Keep an eye out? *Keep an eye out?* He wants to keep an eye out!" the man complained, possibly to the donkey. "For the ronopolisk, whose mere glance can turn a man to stoat!"

Oh, like a basilisk, Scott thought. He knew about basilisks. "Don't you mean 'turn a man to *stone*'?" he asked.

"I said stoat, an' I meant stoat."

Scott glanced at Mick again. "It's a kind o' weasel," Mick whispered.

"I hear tell that the queen of the fairies herself awoke the dreaded ronopolisk," the man continued, "and promised it a great favor if it would only use its hundred noses to hunt down some subject who's displeased her."

Scott sighed. "Well. You'd better get out of here then, 'cause that subject is me. Me and my friend here."

"What?" The man tensed and reined back the donkey's head. Now he lifted a corner of his blindfold and peeked. "But how's that possible? You're just a boy!"

"A *growin'* boy," Mick agreed as he stepped out of the bushes. "So abou' that food—"

The man tossed them one of the donkey's saddlebags before kicking the beast's haunches. Bits of bread and hard cheese spilled out into the road. The donkey lurched into a trot, its ears flicking nervously.

"Protect your eyes, boy, and Fortune preserve you!" the man called as he crested the hill. "May luck be more a lady than that witch Titania!"

Mick and Scott stood on the path and watched the man and his donkey disappear.

"*You* should be good luck, shouldn't you?" Scott asked Mick. "'Cause it kinda seems like you aren't."

"I swear that's the third traveler I've seen wearing a blindfold," said John to Merle and the Queen of England. "What's going on?"

52

"Blindfold or no, it would seem they're all in a great rush to return home," said the queen. "I'm positively bubbling with envy."

Merle sighed. "We're doing the best we can, Your Majesty," he said. "John's son's stuck in Pretannica somewhere too. We thought he and Mick might come back here—"

"To the spot where your so-called rift used to be," finished the queen. "You've said. A more opinionated person than I might wonder why Sir John allowed a child to come to this world in the first place."

John clucked his tongue. "Like I need parenting advice from the British monarchy," he muttered.

Just then Finchbriton returned from scouting the path ahead and chirped a bouncy trio of notes that they'd come to understand meant "all clear." They rose and stretched their legs. The queen, who for complicated reasons was only two feet tall, stepped into John's backpack.

"That's it, then," Merle said as he went through the back-cracking, knee-popping process of getting to his feet. "We head northeast. To Dundalk, maybe, if there is a Dundalk here. And we hire a boat to take us out to the Isle of Man—try to find that pixie castle Prince Fi told us about, so we can get a rift home."

"The castle with the witch and giant henchmen?" said the queen. "I ask merely for clarification."

"To be fair," said John, "they're not really giant. Just human sized."

"I currently fail to see the difference."

"So how d' yeh propose we find our way north if we can't see?" Mick asked the travelers in the buggy. "We haven't any horses or donkeys who know the way, like you lot."

"If yeh knew anythin' about the ronopolisk, yeh wouldn't ask such questions," said the young mother, and she hugged her blindfolded children closer. "Yeh'd just tie somethin' round your eyes and pray to Fortuna."

"Oh, we know all 'bout the ronopolisk," Mick said, glancing at Scott. "Ev'ry man an' his aunt Chatty has been tellin' us 'bout the ronopolisk."

Scott ticked each item off on his fingers. "It has a hundred heads, or maybe a thousand. And each head has a nose and a single eye, and each eye has a different super-power; though to hear everyone tell it, half of them seem to turn you into some kind of weasel. It has two fat legs and a big mouth in its chest, and it's called the ronopolisk because it's like a basilisk and 'rho' means one hundred in Greek or something."

The woman shook her head at them. Or near them, anyway—she was blindfolded.

"I heard it's called the ronopolisk 'cause its great horn is as sharp as Ron, the legendary spear o' King Arthur."

Mick turned to Scott. "That's the first we've heard anythin' about a horn," he said.

"King Arthur had a spear named Ron?"

"It was probably a gift," said Mick. "Are yeh stuck for somethin' to give a visitin' king? Worried it's gonna look like yeh just crammed the first steak knife yeh could find inna nice box? So call it the Great Dagger Carnwennan the Witch Killer or whatever. I'll bet even his chamber-pot had a name."

"Yeah, but Ron?"

They'd been walking a half hour before Merle couldn't keep quiet about it any longer.

"Is it just me," he asked, "or are we seeing an awful lot of weasels all the sudden?"

CHAPTER 5

The ground trembled. The epicenter seemed to move, tracing a slow ring around the spot where they stood.

"Huh," said John. "Earthquake?"

"What did that weasel just say?" asked Merle.

"That wasn't a weasel, that was me. I said, 'Huh. Earthquake?'"

"No, shh," Merle said with a flick of his hand. Then he addressed a weasel that had paused by a thicket. "What did you say?"

"I said, 'Hurry!'" the weasel answered. "It's about to surface again!"

"What is?"

"Ronopolisk!" cried the weasel. Then it was gone.

"Oh, jeez," said Merle, and he threw off his backpack and started fumbling through the pockets. "Close your eyes! Or cover them with something! Your Majesty, maybe you oughtta just zip yourself in."

John shut his eyes tight. "What is it? What's a ronopolisk?"

The tremors reconvened their slow circling path.

"No idea. But it ends in -lisk, and all those people with blindfolds . . . I know at least four different monsters that can kill a man just by lookin' at him funny. What if this is number—"

The earth softened beneath his feet, and in an instant Merle was buried up to his ankles.

"Aah! Help me!"

John grabbed the old man's wrists and pulled him free, and they backed away from a widening sinkhole. Through the sand and grit, three snakelike tendrils unfurled . . . three tendrils topped with piggy noses and bulbous eyes.

"Ooh, don't look at th—" said Merle, before turning into a weasel.

The weasel emerged from the droopy folds of Merle's otherwise empty clothing. "I looked right at them," he said. "Why did I do that?"

John looked only at his own feet until he found the weasel and scooped up his furry noodle of a body. He placed Merle atop his shoulder and backed away from where he imagined the ronopolisk might be. "Finchbriton!" he called.

The finch twittered back.

"Your Majesty! Are you all right back there?"

"Never better. Worry more about yourself, good sir knight."

Good sir knight. That was a nice gesture, John thought.

The ronopolisk was now fully aboveground, and had anyone bothered to look at it they would have seen a body like a six-foot wart, with stamping elephant legs and a gaping snaggletoothed mouth where a waist ought to be. Above the mouth was a horn like a lance, and above the horn were a hundred eyestalks, each with a nose and a big weepy eye.

"WHUH," said the ronopolisk. "BLAR."

John had his sword and the chickadee shield at the ready, and he swiped the former around in crazy eights in front of him.

"Leave us alone! Shoo! Go bother someone else!" John shouted. "YAH!" he added, because the weasel on his shoulder was suddenly not a weasel anymore. The fresh weight almost knocked him backward.

"I looked again," said Merle, or a giant dung fly with Merle's voice. He buzzed down to the ground and botched the landing. "Think it got me with two eyes at once that time."

The beast seemed to be keeping its distance, and sniffing. John heard a hundred stuffy little noses.

"WHUH WHUH CHOHN?" said the ronopolisk.

"I . . . think it just said my name," said John.

"Perhaps it likes your records," said the queen.

"WHUH MERWIN?" the monster added. "WHUH WHUH QUEEN?" Then it charged John. John swung his sword, whiffed, and took the point of the creature's horn in the center of his shield. He was bowled over, caught his heel on an exposed root, and twisted to take the fall on his side and protect his queen. Then a jagged mouth closed over the toe of his boot.

So at least he knew where the monster was. He slashed again and connected this time, and the beast retreated and stomped its feet.

"Merle! You still okay?"

"I was a fly! Then I was three flies. Then three weasels. Then I was trapped in ice for a bit, but that melted and now I think I'm a woman."

"You looked again? Stop looking!"

"I was a fly! I didn't have eyelids!"

John crouched behind his shield—it sounded like the ronopolisk might be charging again—but then he felt flames all around, followed by Finchbriton's whistle.

"WHUH!" said the ronopolisk from some distance away. There was a smell of burned hot dogs. John's sleeve was on fire, and he dropped to his knees to beat it against the ground.

"I looked again!" said Merle. "Accidentally. But I think

60

it changed me back to normal. Am I back to normal?"

The queen peeked out a gap between the zippers. "Apart from the feathers."

"My shield," said John as he groped about. "Where's my shield? I dropped it like an idiot when my sleeve was on fire."

"WHUH WHUH WHUH," said the ronopolisk. It sounded like a chuckle.

John peered through slitted eyes at his feet, then behind him. There was a sturdy tree not far off, and a stupid idea occurred to him, the sort of thing that would only work in the movies. Perfect.

He backed up, forgetting his shield for a moment.

"I was a cloud for a bit," said Merle, "but I'm better now—"

"Shh!" John scolded. He had to listen, he needed quiet.

The ronopolisk snorted, and John listened. It paced back and forth on its fat legs, and John tracked its movement, barely. Then it scuffed the ground and charged, and John trembled as he waited one second, two—

Then he leaped to one side, through a slithering mess of eyestalks, and both felt and heard the horn impale the tree.

"WHUH! RUH!" the monster grunted, heaving backward. The tree creaked and groaned.

John's side ached, his ankle was twisted, he was lying

in a bed of hissing mushrooms. But he came up swinging and moved steadily toward the sounds of struggle until the piñata was in reach. He hacked and slashed, and the monster bellowed. He could have used Merle's help, but Merle was busy being a pile of sausages.

Then the ronopolisk wrenched free, pivoted around, and John was thwacked in the head by the shaft of its horn. Everything went black.

"Sir John!" shouted the queen from his backpack. "Are you awake? Are you alive?"

How much time had passed? John came to and couldn't resist the instinct to open his eyelids. Before he shut them he saw, not a single eye, but rather the cavernous mouth of the ronopolisk looming right above his head.

His sword was still in his hand, but he couldn't move his arm.

The beast had a leg on either side of John's waist, its wrinkly bulk just dripping with stink.

"How do you know our . . . our names?" John panted.

"HUNT YOU."

"Why? Why are you hunting us?"

"MATE! MATE!"

"Oh dear God," said the queen.

"You . . . want to mate with us?"

"QUEEN HAVE MATE!"

"I most certainly do not."

"FAIRY QUEEN! WHUH! FAIRY QUEEN HAVE MATE!"

John let out a breath. "Oh, I . . . I'm sorry," he said. "The fairies are holding your mate. Yes? So you're going to kill us for the fairies."

"MATE!"

John sighed and coughed. "This hero thing . . . I don't like it as much as I thought I might. Finchbriton!"

The little bird whistled from somewhere high.

"Follow my voice! The monster's right on top of me, but the queen is safe! Burn it!"

Finchbriton warbled something, uncertainly.

"Do it! Do it now!"

The ronopolisk seemed to understand and began to back away. But Finchbriton's aim was off too, and he managed by happenstance to torch the monster square in the chest.

John felt singed but not actually aflame, so he reached over with his left hand to grab the sword out of his right, and stabbed. The ronopolisk wailed and slumped to the ground.

"Hey!" said Merle. "Hey, I'm pretty sure I'm normal again! I think I lost a bunch of time, there. What was I? The ronopolisk looks dead."

"So . . . ," said John. "It's safe to open my eyes?"

"Depends on your point of view. I am naked."

"I'm going to give you a moment. Your Majesty? Sorry I fell on you."

"I seem to have survived it. That was . . . you were very brave—to win the day you were willing to be badly burned. We were right to knight you."

John blushed and helped the battered queen out of his backpack. "I thought I was 'too young,'" he told her. "I thought I was just a 'silly pop star.'"

The queen raised an eyebrow. "I only ever said you were too young," she said. "Don't credit me with the whisperings of your own conscience, John."

"Sorry." John smiled. "And thanks."

Finchbriton lit on his shoulder, and when Merle joined them, they all looked down at the dead lumpen figure of the ronopolisk. Its big steak of a tongue lolled out of its mouth; its eyestalks were a tangle of limp pasta. A lot of the eyes were still open, but that didn't seem to matter now.

"Poor dumb thing," John said to himself.

Before long a woman crept toward them through the trees.

"Yeh killed it," she said. She seemed to be trying to hide herself behind some underbrush. "Yeh slew the ronopolisk!"

"Yes," John agreed.

"He slew the ronopolisk!" said the woman to a man who'd just arrived. They were both naked but seemed otherwise happy.

More arrived, all naked, all victims who'd looked the ronopolisk in the eye and spent the past hour as this or that.

"I've heard o' him!" said a man as he pointed at John. "He's the one they call the Chickadee!"

"Why, that's right!" said Merle, grinning.

John winced. "We should probably keep moving," he said.

"Right," said the naked man. "Where are we going?"

CHAPTER 6

Scott and Mick continued to make their way northeast—or what Mick claimed to be northeast, at any rate. The leprechaun seemed to have an innate sense of direction here, despite the lack of sun or stars or moon or compasses.

"I'm getting about ready to rest for the . . . night," said Scott. "Or whatever you want to call it."

Mick gave him a look. "Already? 'S only been nine hours since we woke."

"You keep saying stuff like that. 'Yeh ate fifty minutes ago.' 'That *was* eight hours sleep.' 'We *haven't* been stuck in Pretannica for five hundred years.'"

Mick grunted. "Yeh're starting to sound like your sister."

"You take that back."

"An' was that supposed to have been an impersonation o' me? Yeh sounded Punjabi."

They continued in silence for a minute.

"I'm in a bad mood," said Scott.

"Get out o' town."

"And my feet hurt, because of blisters."

"Sure an' they would."

"Plus the glamour here's been giving me headaches."

"'S like the labors of Hercules, yeh have so much on your plate."

"*Exactly.* That's all I wanted you to say."

Mick glanced around in every direction. "How 'bout we rest for ten minutes, an' I reach out with my glamour to see if any o' Titania's people are gettin' close?"

"You can do that?" asked Scott as he wiggled out of his backpack.

"Takes a bit o' concentration," said Mick, "an' 's difficult to pick anythin' up through all the fuzzy glamour here, but sure."

They sat on a felled tree that was furred over with green moss. Scott kicked off his shoes. Mick exhaled and shut his eyes, but a moment later they snapped open again.

"Oh," he said. Then a net fell on them.

Scott fell off the log and struggled to get out from

under the web of silken ropes. It was held down at eight points with metal weights. As he thrashed, two tall elves stepped out from the shadows, and a third leaped cat-like down from a tree. Each wore a red cap with a pink embroidered dragon.

"Don't leave us in suspense, Finchfather," said the commander. "Are we close? I wait with bated—"

The elf tripped on a tree root and fell face-first onto the net.

"Heh," said Mick.

The other two elves fidgeted and shared an embarrassed glance.

Scott frowned at the elf on the ground. "You guys are usually more . . . you know, *graceful* than that."

The commander got up on his hands and knees. "Forsooth, a dragon's age has passed, and more, since last I lost my footing in this fashion. And then there was a pixie jinx to blame."

"A pixie jinx," said Mick. "Yeh don't say." He seemed to be preoccupied with something he'd spotted in the trees. Scott caught sight of a bit of movement, and squinted up at it—just a bird on a high branch, that was all. Or was there something strange about its back? He strained to make out the shape.

"Polly?" he whispered.

The two elves who were still on their feet slapped their own necks, in unison, as if one were just a mirror image of the other. Each discovered a tiny thorn in his skin. They drew their swords in unison as well, and turned to scan the trees. Then they fell over too.

"Pixies!" said one. A high warbling came from the trees, just as a short-beaked crow with Scott's sister riding it swooped down from the high branch.

"BUG ZAPPER!" screamed Polly, for reasons Scott would have to ask about later. She had a slim straw in her hand, and she used it like a peashooter. Prince Fi followed, astride a second crow and brandishing his sword and shield. The crow's dive skimmed the floundering body of one of the elves, and Fi leaped from the bird's back onto the elf's buttocks. Which he stabbed. The elf made a startled kitten noise and twisted his body to swipe at Fi, but the little prince wasn't where he had been. He dipped his sword briefly into its scabbard and poked the next elf in the thigh.

During all this, the elf commander tried to rise but, having failed to account for the fact that he was now tied at the wrist to his own net, fell forward again. He jerked the net and therefore Scott's head as he did so, and now Scott saw more pixies, pixies he didn't know, creeping through the grass. They had blowguns too, and they

used them to shoot thorns into the commander's arms and neck.

"Pixies! Hear me!" shouted the commander. He anchored the edge of the net with his boot and yanked his arm, ripping the thread that had bound his wrist. "Cease and desist! You are in violation of the Treaty of Nag's Head! An' the trea . . . tready cwearly states—"

He was slurring his speech. He was on his feet now, staring, and seemed to kind of zone out for a second.

"F'got whud I was dalking abou'," he said.

Scott heard another complicated whistle. He'd lost track of Polly, but now she swooped into view again, atop her crow, and buzzed the commander's face. The commander swiveled to strike at her, hit one of his own elves instead, and fell down.

"Hee hee hee hee," said the commander. Then he fell asleep. The elf he'd struck was already quietly snoozing. The remaining elf panicked, stumbled off through the ferns, and ran into a tree.

"We won!" Polly cheered. Her bird landed on the forest floor, and she dismounted and ran to Scott and Mick. "Sorry we weren't here sooner," she said, "but we had to fight a troll, and then we had to make our blowguns and get enough bee stingers and find just the right kinds of flowers and mushrooms. Did you know that there's a poppy here that glows in the dark?"

Scott stared at her. "You're . . . smaller than I remember," he said.

Mick crawled out from under the net while Fi and his brothers gathered around Polly.

"What happened to yeh?" the leprechaun asked her.

"Magic potion, duh," Polly answered.

"Who're your new friends?"

Prince Fi stepped forward. "Mick, Young Master Scott, may I introduce my brothers, Fee, Fo, and Denzil."

The pixies all bowed.

"Enchanted," said Mick. "Literally—I can feel all your pixie auras messin' wi' my glamour."

"Ah, the so-called pixie jinx," said Denzil. "That's naught but an old wives' tale."

"Tell that to the elf there who tripped over a chunk o' tree. Still an' all, yis are a welcome sight an' no foolin'."

"Polly's smaller than she used to be," said Scott. He still hadn't attempted to get himself free of the net.

"Hey, Fi?" said Polly, pointing. "Look." There was a thin stinger stuck in Scott's neck. "Did I do that?"

Mick plucked it out. "Hey now," he said, "what is this? Is he gonna—"

"He will likely fall asleep," said Fi. "We dipped the stingers and filled my scabbard with a . . . recipe known to the pixies. Made from flowers and certain varieties of fungus."

"You peeble are all tiny liddle peeble," Scott told them. Then he took a nap.

CHAPTER 7

The butcher and the baker sat on the grassy hilltop and watched the strangers approach through the twilight. The baker was hogging the telescope, as usual.

"Anyone promising?" the butcher asked him.

"The one in the lead is kind of a little fella," he said. "But he has his own sword an' shield, so that's a good sign. He's got an old man with 'im too. And like twenty naked people."

The butcher wrestled the telescope out of the baker's hands.

"Oi! Give it back!"

"Ho-ho!" said the butcher as he focused on the strangers. "That's weird, innit?"

"Give me back the telescope."

"You think he's some kind o' crazy cult leader or somethin'? He has a sparrow on his shoulder."

"Yeh better send the message, then."

"*You* send the message. I always send the message."

The baker grumbled and got to his feet. He turned the signal device and raised its shutters. A few minutes later he'd sent a message to the men in the tower a mile distant:

M-A-N—A-P-P-R-O-A-C-H-E-S—S-H-O-R-T—
B-L-O-N-D—S-H-O-R-T—H-A-I-R—
N-O—B-E-A-R-D—R-E-D—J-A-C-K-E-T—
S-W-O-R-D—S-H-I-E-L-D—F-O-L-L-O-W-E-D—B-Y—
B-I-R-D—O-L-D—M-A-N—
T-W-E-N-T-Y—N-A-K-E-D—P-E-O-P-L-E

"I thought they just called him the Chickadee because there's one painted on his shield," said one of the naked people.

"A common mistake!" said Merle. "He was raised by chickadees and painted that portrait in honor of his dear departed mother."

"Aw," said someone.

John could feel the queen fidgeting in the backpack, so he guessed what she was going to ask before she asked it.

"I'd like to lie down in your hood again for a while," she said. "All this standing aggravates my sciatica."

John helped her out of the sack and into the hood of his jacket. She reclined in it like a baby in a sling.

"So why does the bird go everywhere he goes?" asked another naked person. "That's not a chickadee, that's a chaffinch."

"Friend of the family," said Merle.

"Ohhhh," said the naked people.

"I think . . . ," John said to the queen. "I think after this is all over I'm going to try *not* being famous for a while."

"Good luck with that," the queen answered. "One does not simply decide, one has to ask for permission. You're their paper doll now."

"Merle would say it's because I'm a changeling. It's my fairyness that makes people want to tell stories about me. When I was younger, you know . . . I was confused about who I was, what I wanted. And when I was confused I couldn't get hired singing telegrams. Then I figure out a few things, and *bam*—I'm magic."

"When I was a very little girl, I thought everyone was famous," said the queen with a smile. "Everyone *I* knew was, after all."

"At least you didn't choose it. I *chose* it. And then I made some other choices I shouldn't have."

Merle came alongside them. "Hey, have you noticed?" he said. "There's a couple guys on the road ahead."

William Baker kept a hand on John's back as he steered him toward the Village of Reek. Billy Butcher was so afraid of being caught leering at the naked ladies that he didn't look at them at all, and instead smiled uncomfortably at the tiny old woman sitting in John's hood.

"Yeh have a crown," Billy told the tiny woman.

"Yes. My former captors made me this crown. I think it was a joke to them."

Billy chewed his cheek. "Oh. Why are yeh still wearin' it, then?"

"Because it is not a joke to me. I am the Queen of England."

Billy was a reluctant liar, so he mostly pretended to believe other liars as a kind of professional courtesy.

"Oh right," he told the queen, nodding. "Didn't recognize yeh."

Merle caught up to them. "I'd like to hear some more about this Chosen One prophecy," he said. "Who made it? How long ago? And what makes you think my friend here is your guy?"

"Ah," said the baker. "I'd better let one o' the village elders handle all that. Declan Sage . . . he's the, ah, current keeper o' the scroll."

"There's a scroll? What's it say?"

"Yes, I'm awfully curious too, obviously," said John. "Can't you at least tell us more about this 'evil that has befallen the land' business?"

"There now," said the baker. "I never said 'evil.' I said

77

'nuisance.' Didn't I, Billy?"

Billy winced and belched, and whether or not this amounted to an endorsement was anyone's guess.

"All right then, a nuisance, but what sort of nuisance?"

"Declan Sage'll answer everythin'."

They approached the village gates. The city's wall was three stories tall, made of stripped and tightly packed tree trunks like telephone poles. Woven throughout these poles were bands of wrought iron. Something behind the wall was burning, its soot craning upward like a warty black neck.

"Oi there!" shouted a guard atop a wooden tower. "Is that you, William?"

"'Tis. An' I have with me the Chosen One!"

The guard had an expression that was hard to decipher. "You don't say. Better open up, then." He heaved himself off his stool and started down the stairs.

"Mister Chickadee?" asked one of the women. "Do you suppose your new friends might find us some clothes before we enter town?"

"Oh hey," Billy said to John. "You're the Chickadee? I heard o' you. Everyone's talkin' 'bout those people yeh saved from a tribe o' murderous brownies."

John smiled wanly as they waited outside the gates while one of the guards fetched a stack of blankets, which were passed around. Then two guards opened the gates with a flourish, and the village introduced itself.

Once again, John had to remind himself that, despite being trapped for all intents and purposes in a medieval fantasy movie, he hadn't actually traveled in time. It was the twenty-first century here too, and the thatched-roof huts and rancid living conditions he'd expected quickly gave way to a clean and pleasant little town with paved roads and blandly boxy, almost modern-looking houses.

"Welcome to the Village of Reek!" said William.

People bustled about with baskets, a man pushed a cart laden with flowers, children paused in their play to openly stare at John and Merle and the rest.

"Perhaps some of the townsfolk can take these nice people someplace to . . . freshen up," said John.

"Yeah," said William. "Hey! Mary! Can yeh take this lot wi' the blankets over to see Millie Tailor? An' then maybe to the bathhouse."

"I should like to freshen up myself," said the queen, so she was helped out of John's pack.

"Makes me nervous even letting her out of our sight," Merle muttered to Finchbriton. "Stay with her, would you?" Finchbriton whistled and perched atop the queen's crown as Merle added, "Mary! It's Mary, right? Treat the little woman good, okay? She's a queen where she's from."

The queen looked over her shoulder and gave them

a meaningful look. "I would prefer that no one make a fuss," she said, "as I trust we won't be staying long?"

Soon John and Merle were alone with the butcher and baker. "Just this way," said the baker with a wave.

They passed a skinny busker who played his lute and sang about the meadow being a lady, or a lady being a meadow, or some such. But William snapped his fingers when he thought Merle wasn't looking, and the busker nodded, cut his song short, and began another:

> "Little dragon, little dragon—you're alone, they say,
> and lonely,
> And you've pillaged our poor village now for oh!
> so many seasons.
> But despite your size and feeble eyes, you nonetheless
> can only
> By the Chosen One be beaten, for inconsequential
> reasons."

"Is that your 'nuisance'?" said Merle. "You guys have a dragon problem?"

"Almost there," said William.

A thin-wheeled wagon that looked something like a go-kart with an espresso machine attached putt-putted by. The man piloting it tipped his cap.

"Nice!" said Merle. "Was that a steam-powered car?"

"That was a completely reckless waste o' time, was what that was," said William with a sneer. "The thing's useless on rough roads, an' it only takes twenty minutes to walk the length and breadth o' Reek, so what's it good for?"

"The ladies like it," observed Billy.

John turned his head to follow the car's path and spied, through gaps and alleys, the source of the tower of smoke they'd seen outside the village wall. He couldn't tell what it had been, but the ruins of it glowed a furious purple that snapped and cursed and bent the air.

"That looks bad," said John. "Did this dragon do that? Was anybody hurt?"

Billy coughed. William acted as if he had to search to see what John was asking about, acted as if he was unimpressed, as if he'd forgotten all about the pile of smoldering rubble, acted in a manner that John had to say, charitably, was maybe not the best performance he'd ever seen.

"Oh what, that?" asked William. "That's always been there. I don't even see it anymore."

"It's funny," Billy said, "what yeh only notice abou' your town when people visit."

John and Merle shared a look.

"Yeah," Merle said. "I mean, I lived in New York for fifteen years and I only ever looked at the Statue of

Liberty when family came. Course, it was never actually *on fire—*"

They were approaching a fairly plain octagonal building made of stucco. "Here we are," said William under a sign that read REEK PUBLIC HOUSE NUMBER TWO.

"Well, that's a real nice name," said Merle.

They entered into a great room filled with mismatching tables, benches, chairs. A chandelier of antlers hung from a rough wooden rafter. The floor was a patchwork of raw white planks, covered with sawdust, and the whole pub smelled like shop class.

A few men and women sat in here, drinking or smoking, but with a jerk of William's head they hustled out by the back door. They were scarcely gone a second before an older man entered from an adjoining room, draped in uncomfortable-looking burlap robes festooned with coins and charms and bangles. He sounded like a wind chime when he moved.

This man gasped, faintly, and looked seriously at John. "There he is," he said. Then he acknowledged Merle as well and added, "Gentlemen. I am Declan Sage, historian of the Village of Reek. Thank you for agreeing to come."

"Of course," said John.

"Centuries ago, our simple village was a happy place. Then the Gloria came, and the world withered and became a dusky fairy island. And we were confined to this twilight bubble in a great black sea of nothing."

"Right," said Merle. There was something about this old man and his practiced shtick that was rubbing Merle the wrong way. It felt rather a lot, he realized, like passing a mirror and catching sight of your own unflattering reflection.

"The world continued ever so slowly to shrivel and die," said Declan, "and so the Fay grew angry, and then bold. They goaded the magical creatures against us and raised a dragon on the highest peak of the Black Stacks. But one day it is prophesied that a Chosen One will lead us. A stranger. And see here—it's you."

He unrolled a scroll of brown paper to show them a drawing of what could have been John, followed by what could have been Merle, followed by what was definitely a bunch of naked people. John raised his eyebrows.

"That is awfully specific," he said.

Declan unrolled the scroll a bit more. "And here you are again, after you're clothed in a fine suit of armor once worn by the great Lancelot himself at the Battle of Camlann, and waiting hollow all these centuries for the Chosen One to claim it. Then you will choose your weapons and ride up the mountain to rid this land of a garden-variety run-of-the-mill dragon."

This dragon was pink, and John edged forward in his chair. "Saxbriton?"

"No, no," said Declan with a smile. "Goodness, no. No no no."

"No," agreed William.

"Yes or no? Out with it," said Merle.

"No. No," said Declan. "I think the Great Dragon Saxbriton is in Orkney this time of year, is she not, lads?"

"Orkney." Billy hiccuped.

"Oh," said John, sitting back.

Declan eyed him. "You . . . seem disappointed," he said.

"Oh, not . . . *disappointed*, exactly. It's just that I was planning on slaying Saxbriton at some point anyway . . . so. I'm sure your dragon is great."

Declan exchanged a furtive glance with Billy and William. "Well now," he said. "The fact of the matter is that we don't know for *certain* that it's not Saxbriton—"

"Oh com' on," Merle growled. "It is or it isn't?"

"Hard to say. Hard to say—she's in and out so fast when she attacks the village . . . I don't know that any of us has ever gotten a good look at her."

Merle leaned closer to John. "Notice that it's a *she*, now," he said.

"She may be larger than we realize," said Declan, ignoring Merle. "And I think it's safe to say that the reports of Saxbriton's great size are probably exaggerated anyway. I mean, *really*."

Declan chuckled and passed the chuckle like a stack of party hats to William and Billy. They all made a great show of it.

"An' . . . heh . . . an' none o' the *other* dragon slayers ever came back, so *they* couldn't tell us what she looked—" said Billy, right up until William elbowed him in the ribs.

"Well, my friend and I will discuss it and get back to—" said Merle, but John was already standing.

"Gentlemen," he announced, "I will slay your dragon!" Then the men cheered, and there was much backslapping, and John signed some piece of paper, and happy villagers stormed the pub.

CHAPTER 8

After the villagers rushed into the pub, they seemed to make a point of separating Merle and John, and they carried the younger man off on their shoulders while a couple of nice-looking young women cornered Merle and tried to convince him that they liked his beard.

"Oh, you do not," said Merle. "Where'd my friend go?"

"The one with no beard?" said the short one. "They probably took him to the armory for a fitting."

"Right. And then off to shrive himself and pray all night over his new armor?"

"I don't know what that word means," she said.

"They'll probably want him to start up the mountain right away," the other woman told him. "You know . . . element o' surprise and all that."

Merle was already moving for the door. "Right. Someone point me toward the armory? Thanks." He pushed his way through to the street, asking for directions along the way. The armory was another newish-looking building up the road. It had a stone foundation but was otherwise similar to all the other indifferently built plaster people boxes that lined this main thoroughfare. Not one of them looked more than five years old. These were sand castles.

John rounded the corner of the armory, atop a horse, wearing a full suit of plate armor. This armor was dazzling—it should have had its own segment on the Home Shopping Network. It should have had a spokesmodel introducing it to you at a boat show.

"Uh-uh," said Merle. "Nope. No way. You are not going to face a dragon dressed like that."

"What's wrong with it?" asked John as he frowned down at his breastplate. "I thought it looked great."

"That's the problem. This is parade armor. Not fighting armor. No one ever won the day by being the best looking."

"They said Lancelot himself wore this."

"Yeah, they seem to be saying a lot of things," Merle groused as he looked sideways at the townsfolk. "But trust me, I knew Lancelot."

A nearby villager leaned into another.

"Old man says he knew Lancelot."

Merle took John's horse by the reins and turned them

around. "Lancelot wouldn't have been caught dead in this. Whereas I think it's more than likely you will be caught dead in this."

John was petulantly silent.

"Look," Merle added, "even if Lancelot did wear this armor, which he didn't, who cares? It wasn't the clothes that made the man, and *he* never would have worn a thousand-year-old antique just 'cause it belonged to someone's famous grandpa."

John sighed. "Fine, help me down."

Merle helped John dismount his horse and waited patiently as he robot-walked back inside the armory.

The startled armorer looked up from his sweeping.

"You!" Merle said. "You put my friend in this lemon?"

The man scowled while Merle helped John with his gauntlets. "What? This is the nicest suit I have."

"Yeah. It's so nice you'll wanna make sure you clean all the dead knight out of it before you hang it back up again. It's not about who's prettiest, you know."

The blacksmith flapped his lips like a horse, but he had no answer.

"You keep saying that," John told Merle. "You forget that your plan to win us those merrow's caps was based *entirely* on me being prettiest."

"Okay, but . . . you see this—this hood ornament?" Merle asked him with a wave of his hand at the brass lion head on John's breastplate. "Or these . . . what are these, dolphins? Or this scrollwork? All of these would stop a sword, or a claw."

John struggled with a buckle and smiled apologetically at the blacksmith. "Isn't that the point, Merle?"

"We want to *deflect blows,* not connect with them. If Saxbriton gets a good toehold on any piece of your armor, she's gonna tear it right off."

"Look, old man," said the smith. "Who do you think you are?"

"I am *Merlin.* Yeah. *That* Merlin. And I've seen enough dead knights for three lifetimes. Bring us something plain, sleek. None of your pimped-out suits. This one may as well have vanity plates."

"I only understand half of what you say," the blacksmith answered as he shuffled off.

"Well, I don't care how it looks," said John, and he was such a good actor that only Merle knew he was lying. "So long as it's thick."

"No, no. We want you built for speed. A direct hit from Saxbriton's talon, or her tail? It's gonna crush you no matter what you're wearing. The full force of her fiery breath? It'll boil you right in your kettle."

"You should be a football coach. One locker-room pep talk and your players would hang themselves with their own towels."

Merle pressed closer and lowered his voice. "I don't like this, John. I know what a good con looks like. I was a good con man—making everyone think I was a wizard, putting Arthur on the throne. Have you really looked at the buildings in this town? They're nearly all new. And they're built like everyone's just waiting for the neighborhood bully to come knock them down again."

"I agree," said John. "Because the Village of Reek has a *really serious* dragon problem. I think it's Saxbriton!"

"And you're . . . you think you're ready to face her? Already?"

"Look, we've been assuming we'd have to fight her after she came to Earth. But why wait? Why not take the fight to her, in her own home—catch her off guard? You saw that prophecy of theirs. I'm supposed to do this now."

"Yeah . . . about that. I'm not convinced that scroll's legit."

John coughed. "You can't be serious. That wasn't some vague fortune cookie, Merle, that was a painting of two men and a bird and a dozen nudes."

"I just wonder . . . what if they decorated the scroll *after* they saw us? Somehow."

"When? When was there time, Merle?"

Merle bit his nail, frowning. "Just 'cause I don't know how the trick was done doesn't mean it's not a trick. I don't know how they saw ladies in half either."

John smiled. "I appreciate your concern, but . . . this feels right. I'm going to do it."

"And this thing you're going to do . . . ," said Merle as he studied John's radiant face, "this is just about prophecy, and strategy? Not about you feeling down all week?"

John's face fell a little. He glanced over at the blacksmith, who went abruptly back to his sweeping.

"Saxbriton has to be beaten. Everyone agrees on this. I'll be saving two worlds if I beat her."

"Unlike the ronopolisk," Merle said, nodding. "Or that tree person you hacked to bits, then felt bad about."

John sat heavily on a stool, still weighed down by scraps of armor. "The ronopolisk was just some poor dumb thing."

"If you hadn't killed it, I'd still be a rock or a toadstool or whatever I was," said Merle. "All those people in your new fan club would still be weasels."

"I know it. I know it. But listen. These past ten years, people have been all too happy to join my fan club. Before I was killing monsters and saving queens. Back when I was only pretending to kill monsters, and saving actresses, and singing about it."

Merle smirked. "Is this the part where the action star says it's firefighters who're the real heroes?"

"Well?" said John. "Aren't they? Look, there's nothing wrong with playing dress-up, but I left my family to play dress-up. That's what I got rich and famous for. And now this Chickadee business, and I can't feel good about that either. But Saxbriton—that's a slam dunk. Or a . . . home run, or a touchdown, or some other American sports metaphor."

"You wanna talk mistakes, John?" Merle snarled suddenly. He paced the floor. "I tore the *universe in two*. I made the Gloria happen with my time machines and separated magic from the world and doomed millions to die in this . . . oversized terrarium! Emily said so—you heard her."

"Emily might be wrong," said John.

"Emily might be amphibious too, but nothing we've seen so far suggests either is true."

The armory was quiet for a moment.

"Look, John," said Merle. "I want a big win as much as anyone, but . . . we need a live actor more than a dead hero right now—you get that, right?"

John nodded. "You'd better help me pick a suit of armor, then."

CHAPTER 9

Scott awoke to see the blue-dappled canopies of Pretannican trees passing overhead. The leaves gently waved to him. He gently waved back.

He was lying down. He was also moving. He tried to reconcile these two things as he lifted his head and found that Mick was carrying his feet.

"Ah, yeh're up," said the leprechaun, smiling. "Aces. Think yeh might be willin' to carry yourself for a bit?"

No sooner had Scott become aware that he might actually be suspended several inches above the ground atop the heads of pixies than he heard Fi call, "Brothers! Time to execute maneuver the Dainty Butterfly!"

"The Dainty Butterfly?" Scott asked Mick.

"They let your sister name it."

"Where is Polly?"

"I was holding up your head," said Polly. Scott still

couldn't see her. "But now you're holding up your head."

"On my mark, brothers!" said Fi. "Mark!"

Scott's whole body wobbled a bit, then listed a bit to the right and dropped abruptly onto the dirt.

"Ow," said Scott.

Fi appeared at Scott's side as he lifted himself up onto his elbow. "My apologies, Scott," said Fi. "That was not a successful run-through of the Dainty Butterfly."

"That's okay," said Scott, getting up. "What happened? Why did I fall asleep?"

"You succumbed to an errant thorn that was laced with a potion called the Dreaming Draught."

"Did Polly name that, too?"

Fi straightened. "No. It was discovered and named by the legendary pixie hero Cornwallace, my great-great-great-great-grandfather."

"Oh. Does my sister have tiny wings growing out of her back?"

"You ask a lot of questions," said Polly. "Did you see me riding that bird?"

"Uh-huh."

"Wasn't I amazing?"

"Sure."

Now that he was upright, Scott could return the favor by carrying Polly, Fi, and Fo on his shoulders, and Mick in his backpack. Denzil sat atop Mick's head as Finchbriton once had, and Scott could hear the two of them talking politics or something. Fee had a personal issue with being carried, and insisted on sprinting alongside Scott and pretending that he wasn't getting tired.

"How did you guys even find us?" Scott asked.

"We asked the birds," said Fi. "Most of them are incurable gossips. Jackdaws and other crows particularly have always shown a special interest in the movements of men."

"They said that you and Mick were almost the only travelers around," said Polly. "Everyone else is home playing Monopoly."

"Everyone else is home *hiding* from the *ronopolisk*," Fi corrected.

"Do the birds know anything about Dad and Merle and Finchbriton?" said Scott.

"Some thought they might have entered a town many miles to the southwest. The birds lost track of them there."

"Do you smell that?" asked Fo. "We're getting nearer to the sea."

Scott paused and asked Mick to hand him the map. He still had the one Emily had passed out not so long ago in a London basement. It featured, among other things, England, Ireland, Scotland, and Wales—and a circular border that showed just how much of these lands still existed, here in Pretannica. Anything outside of the bubble had been consumed by the magical nothing of the Gloria Wall.

"So that pixie witch . . . ," Scott began, holding the map so they all could see.

"Fray," said Fi.

"Right. Where's Fray's island exactly?"

"It is too small to appear on this map," said Fi. "But we will find it in the Irish Sea, just south of the Isle of Man."

"Sorta right smack in the middle," said Scott.

Polly screwed up her eyes. "Ooh," she said, fanning her face. "Ooh, I'm remembering something important. What was it? Something Erno left a message about on Merle's watch thing."

Scott gave her a minute. Finally he said, "Before we left for Pretannica he was going on and on about that page from the old Freeman's Handbook—"

"Yes! That's it! The page was the start of some instructions on how to draw something—"

"The Sickle and Spoon," said Scott. "The Freeman's symbol."

"Yeah, but all it said was to start by tracing a circle . . ."

"And then find the center of the circle," said Scott. "Then that was it."

"The circle on that map reminded me," said Polly. "Erno left some message about how the center wasn't where it

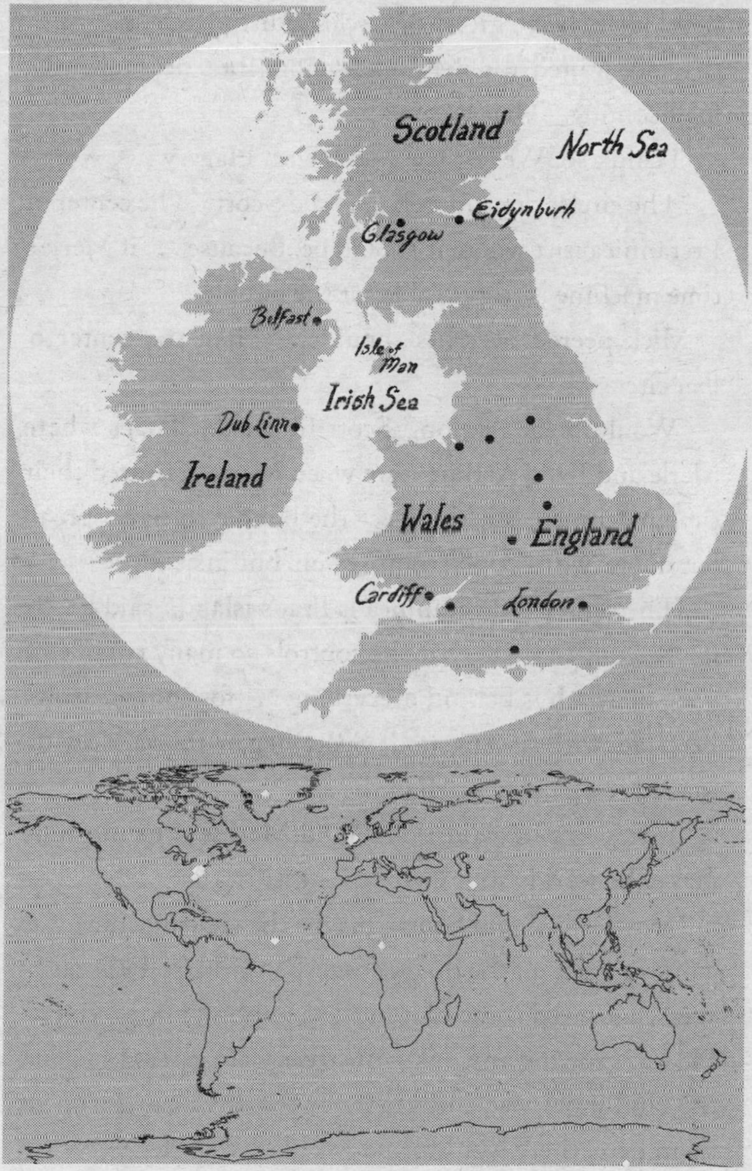

Scotland

North Sea

Glasgow · Eidynburh

Belfast ·

Isle of
Man

Irish Sea

Dub Linn ·

Ireland

Wales · England

Cardiff · London ·

should have been. How the circles didn't match up."

Scott waited for her to say more, but no more was forthcoming. "That was it?"

"I think so. We left the watch with Harvey."

"The circles don't match up," said Scott. "The center of Pretannica isn't where it should be. Because . . . if Merle's time machine is responsible for the bubble . . ."

Mick peered over his shoulder. "Then the center o' *that* circle . . ."

"Would be at Avalon," Scott finished. "That's where Merle and King Arthur were when Merle activated their time machines. You'd expect the bubble to have spread out in every direction from Avalon, but instead—"

"The center of Pretannica is Fray's island," said Fi. "Is it any wonder, then, that she controls so many rifts?"

"The witch is behind everything . . . for some reason," Fee said with a slow nod. Scott began to walk again, toward the pickley smell of the sea.

"I don't get it," said Polly. "Did Merle's time machine make the worlds split up, or didn't it?"

"Maybe . . . ," said Scott, "maybe the time machine was going to erase all the magic from the world, so Fray cast a spell that saved some of it inside a bubble? I don't know." He was growing anxious—the trees were getting sparser, the land more wet and grassy. If the elves caught up to them here, there wouldn't be any place to hide.

"There," said Denzil, pointing, "the sea awaits! We shall convince some friendly seagulls to give us passage, and—"

"Scott an' I can't hitch a ride on no bird," Mick interrupted.

"Not on the outside of one, anyway," Scott murmured. He stepped lightly across the loose cobblestone of the beach, to the water's edge.

"Then we shall build a raft!" said Denzil. "And name her for beautiful Morenwyn! She will carry us across the waters—"

"What *is* that?" said Scott, squinting. The Irish Sea lapped at the pebbly beach, and a low gray mist seemed to roll in and out with the waves. Out on the water, through the mist, a white shape drifted like a ghost.

Then, some distance behind them, a horn blew.

"Aw, bippity Christmas," said Mick.

Scott turned his head and said, "Bippity Christmas?"

"Beg your pardon," Mick said. "Back when I was a prisoner o' Goodco I took to inventin' swears. As a hobby. But that horn yis just heard? That's the horn o' Oberon. His troopin' fairies are closin' in."

Scott turned and tried to see. "Probably those three we left sleeping in the forest, right?"

"If it were only them three, they wouldn't need the horn. They're calling to another regiment."

Scott thought he could see elves back near the tree line. And another group, descending from the north . . . were they on horseback?

On the water, the spectral shape came ever closer. Now Scott could see it was a boat—long and lean, without a sail, but draped with languid garlands of silk.

He threw his arm high and waved to it, sending Fo flailing to keep his place on Scott's shoulder. But the gesture might well have been pointless—the boat seemed to be heading right for them, whether they liked it or not.

"I don't see any people," said Polly.

"Plenty o' people behind us, lass," Mick answered. "Those three soldiers who netted us, plus another ten on horses. I think they see us."

The boat nosed up onto the shore and stopped. It was large enough for a crew of six or seven, but it appeared to be empty.

"Well," said Scott, casting his attention back and forth, "this is a good sign, right? In the old Arthurian stories it was always a good thing when a mystery boat showed up."

"Always?" said Mick.

"Always. Well, except for when it was a really bad thing."

An arrow shattered against the stones at their feet.

"Boat! Boat!" shouted Polly.

Scott threw his wobbly self over the side of the craft and reached out for Fee, who suddenly didn't mind being carried so much after all. The moment they were all aboard, the boat shuddered, and with a scrape it pushed itself off the rocks and into the surf.

Another arrow landed, and a third, and then it was as if the sky opened up and poured. Arrows dashed against the rocks, and roiled the water, and lodged their silver teeth in the hull of the boat. In a panic Scott dislodged his backpack, gathered up his sister and Mick and all the pixies he could see, and crouched over them, making his back a shield.

"Lemme go, lad!" said Mick.

Something struck Scott. It took a moment to realize that an arrow had only gone through the hood of his jacket.

"I mean it! Yeh're too young to be takin' arrows for the likes o' me!"

Scott was considering how lucky that was, an arrow right through his hood, when another grazed his arm and drew blood. He hissed from the pain.

Mick fought his way free and threw himself across Scott's back, but the worst had passed. The last arrow to hit the boat landed just shy of Scott's foot. The rest plunked into the water off the stern, and soon those sounds dwindled and died altogether. Scott raised his head and found he couldn't even see the elves on the shore anymore.

He unclenched his body and fell backward onto his seat. Polly and the pixies were just staring at him.

"That was uncalled for, boy," said Fee. "The youngest son of Denzil does not need protecting—"

"Shut your ungrateful mouth, Fee," said Denzil, and Fee looked down. Denzil nodded at Scott. "Son, I'm too wise to hope that I may one day repay this good turn— only a fool hopes for calamity. But then, your sister tells me that calamity seems to follow you wherever you go."

"Aw, that's not calamity," said the ghost of Haskoll. He'd just appeared at the bow of the boat. "That's me."

"Same thing," Scott muttered.

"What's that, son?" asked Denzil.

Scott shook his head. "Nothing," he said. Of course nobody else noticed Haskoll. "We're not really keeping score, are we?" he added. "You guys got us out of that net."

Mick socked Scott in the arm and smiled at him. Fi bowed. Polly hugged his wrist.

"Look at that," said Haskoll. "All the action figures think you're the best little boy. It's like the end of one of those Toy Story movies."

Polly looked up at Scott. "I'm sorry," she said, "for . . . everything I've ever done or said to you my whole life."

Scott laughed. "Oh, come on, what do you mean?"

"You know . . . calling you a dork, and making you

always watch what I wanna watch, and stealing from your piggy bank all the time in tiny amounts so you won't notice."

Scott frowned. "I didn't know about that last thing."

The big moment passed, and soon everyone was coughing self-consciously and wondering where to look. The boat bounced briskly over the choppy waves. There was no mast, no sail, no oars.

Haskoll was pretending to be seasick over the bow.

"So," said Fo. "Where do you suppose we're going?"

CHAPTER 10

"This is absurd," said the queen. "I was given to believe the whole motivation for rescuing me was so that I could knight an army to fight this Saxbriton. And now we delay so that you might chase after her by yourself?"

"She's got it," said Merle. "That's it entirely."

Billy Butcher and William Baker waited at the village gates, shifting and scratching astride their mules. John sat his horse high on the stirrups, looking uncomfortable. They'd found Merle a pony.

"And could these possibly be the best steeds available?" continued the queen. "Look at the teeth on that one. It's twenty years old if it's a day. No. As your queen, I forbid you to go."

A crowd of villagers had gathered to see them off, and the tiny Queen Elizabeth II stood at the front, holding them at bay with the outsized force of her personality.

John tightened up inside his metal suit—this was like getting told off by his mom in front of his friends.

"He has a good feeling about it, Your Majesty," said Merle.

"Well, then. Splendid. Clearly I wasn't seeing the whole picture. That's what the British Empire was built on, you know—our excellent *feelings*."

"Your Majesty," said John. He shifted, and you could tell he wanted to dismount and kneel before his queen but was uncertain he could manage it in full armor without humiliating himself. "Your Majesty, if you forbid me to go, I won't go. Please don't forbid me."

The queen stood watching him for a minute with a face like a shut purse. The Village of Reek held its collective breath.

"You will come back," she told him. "I have one of your dreadful songs stuck in my head and I can't remember the end of it. If you don't return—*both* of you—then I shall die in this place with only the first verse of 'Love Is a Song Your Heart Sings' to keep me company. God help me, I will haunt your descendants."

John smiled. "Thank you, Your Majesty. Finchbriton! Take good care of her."

"Nonsense. You'll need the bird far more than I. The people of this town will protect me."

"The people of this town would rather trick someone

else into whitewashing that fence," said Merle. "They couldn't protect themselves from a bad haircut." He nodded at the Village of Reek. "No offense."

The Village of Reek shrugged. "None taken," said someone.

Merle and John reined their mounts around. John supposed that the villagers had intended to cheer or something as they left, but the mood had been spoiled, and now walking his horse to the village gates with five hundred people staring silently at his backside was unnerving. He was glad when the gates closed behind him and he didn't have to think about them anymore.

His armor now was as plain as a suit could be, all bald plates and convex curves. And Merle had insisted it be polished with hog fat, so John smelled like a sandwich. His own sword was at his side, freshly sharpened.

Merle carried John's spear so John could save his arm for battle. John felt bad for the old man, who kept passing it uncomfortably from hand to hand.

"You still have the chickadee shield," said Merle. "Didn't they offer you a new one?"

They had, in fact. John had joked and complained about the chickadee until the blacksmith handed him a replacement, which John then sheepishly declined. Someone who believed in him had given him this shield.

"No," John told Merle. "I guess I'm stuck with it."

They proceeded for a while in silence. But Billy Butcher's guilty conscience couldn't abide long silences, so he filled it with a lot of chatter about the countryside.

"So that was the last o' the Aching Foothills," he said. "I'll tell yeh when we get near Hag's Glen, 'cause ych'll want to keep an eye out for hags."

"Mm-hm" was all John said in reply.

"After that it's the Devil's Ladder, which isn't a proper ladder at all—'s more like a pass between the mountains. But it's full of loose rocks and a real tricky climb."

"These are super names," said Merle. "I'm surprised you guys aren't getting more tourists."

"If you like names, yeh'll find this interestin'," Billy continued. "I fancy yeh've noticed how damp this gully is—this one we're ridin' through now—an' yeh're probably wonderin', 'Billy, why so damp?' It just so happens that the constant dampness is one of the great unexplained mysteries o' County Kerry, but it's why they call this gully the Harpy's Armpit! That, an' it bein' infested with harpies."

"Ah," said John. "What?"

There was a clamor in the thickets all around them, and then the air pulsed with flapping bodies—leathery old women with wings for arms and raptors' feet. John brought his hand to his sword, and Merle fumbled with the spear.

"BLEAH!" called one of the harpies, and then they were all saying it, "BLEAH! BLEAH!" and "BLECH!" and "PUH! PUH! PUH!" like they were trying to spit but hadn't the juice for it.

"As yeh probably know, Irish harpies are mostly harmless," said Billy as the creatures began to settle down and disappear once more into the bushes. "They've got only a rudem . . . rude . . . what is it again, William?"

"Rudimentary," said William.

"A rudimentary intelligence, an' their language has only words for disgust an' for talking abou' their grandchildren. Careful, now, as we descend a bit into the marshy fen known only as the Bladder."

They sank into a muddy moor, their animals' hooves going *spluck spluck spluck* until they rose up the grassy bank on the opposite side and entered Hag's Glen.

Hag's Glen was green and lush (and damp) and not nearly the forbidding place that John had expected. The grass and brush stopped abruptly about halfway up the peak, however, and above that the mountain looked about as inviting as a wet campfire.

"It's black as a cinder," John whispered.

"A natural coloration," Billy told them, "owin' to the large coal deposits that are found here."

John and Merle gave him a look.

"All right, yeah," Billy admitted. "The dragon did it."

They fell into a thick silence after that, and passage through the glen was uneventful—they only saw two hags and were at the base of the Devil's Ladder before anyone spoke again.

"This is where we must stop," said William. "For Billy Butcher an' I are not Chosen Ones, and may go no farther."

"Uh-huh," said Merle. "Bet you're gonna let *me* keep going though, right?"

William and Billy looked at each other and shrugged.

"Well . . . ," said Billy. "Yeh *were* on the scroll."

"Yeah," William agreed, "there yeh go. So it should be okay."

They all stared at one another for a moment before Merle steered his pony away.

"All right, I'm through with these guys," he said. "I swear they're making me stupider."

John lobbed a weak smile at them and followed.

"I hope yeh win!" Billy called after them.

CHAPTER 11

The higher they climbed, the harder it was to breathe. That wasn't unusual in itself, but the air on the black mountain seemed to be getting thicker, not thinner, and they kept clearing their throats like they were trying to unstop a clogged drain.

"It doesn't feel like breathing," John rasped. "It feels like I'm pushing a sofa up and down a flight of stairs."

"Mmm," said Merle.

"The sofa in this metaphor," John added, "has recently been set on fire."

Merle coughed.

"Is that how it feels to you too? Like pushing a burned sofa?"

"Yes," said Merle. "Which is why I'm trying not to talk so much."

Merle's pony had quailed at climbing the Devil's

Ladder, so he'd left it tied to a rock. Now he was helping lead John's horse to the crest of this steep, char-black shambles. Even John was quieted by a prolonged shush of loose shale sliding down the mountain.

They were to veer up to the peak of Carrauntoohil now, so they took a moment to wince at it. There was dark weather here—a weightless fall of flaky ash that stuck to hair, lips, the greasy polish on John's armor. Without a word they leaned into it and started up the black stack.

After a while John whispered, "So what do you know about dragons?"

"Not much," said Merle. "Mostly just what I've read in old bestiaries. The same books that also claim that crocodile dung makes a good wrinkle cream, so I never took them too seriously."

"I guess I was hoping that they all had a weak spot, maybe. Like in *The Hobbit*."

"The old books say they're afraid of leopards," Merle offered. "That's a weakness."

"Well. You might have mentioned that back at the village. We could have borrowed one."

"Okay, here's something that might be useful," said Merle. "All the stories I ever heard about knights slaying dragons started out the same way: the dragon breathes flame, the knight ducks behind his shield or a big rock or whatever, and then the dragon closes in to attack with its teeth and claws."

John coughed. "I don't think that anecdote is as useful as you do," he said.

"But listen—why wouldn't a dragon just keep breathing fire if it could? Eventually that rock's gonna melt, or the knight'll be forced to drop his shield. So maybe a dragon can't just keep breathing fire? Maybe it needs some time to recover."

They were startled by a low hiss, but when they looked up it was just a vulture perched atop a crag—a snowy-headed, red-feathered little monster. The hiss was echoed below, and John and Merle turned to see twelve more vultures crowding the path behind them.

"Go away," Merle said through his teeth. "We're not dead yet."

The birds scowled back, a dozen wrinkled little white heads. They reminded John of certain matinee audiences he'd played to in the old days.

The vultures were still behind them when they neared the jagged lip of the summit, where there was a vast bowl like a dormant volcano.

It was difficult to see when the air was this choked with soot and sulfur. But the bowl appeared to be filled with blackened tree trunks and a knee-high sand trap of cinders and ash. There were bones too. Little steeples of bones, jutting here and there out of the dust—some still flecked with bits of charred flesh.

"This is reminding me," John whispered. "When we're safely home again, I need to clean my oven."

Merle frowned at him. "Was that a quip? Are you quipping now?"

"Can't help it. It's all I know. I've spent the better part of our climb trying to think of something funny to say after I kill Saxbriton."

"What've you come up with?"

"Nothing good. I shouldn't have brought it up."

"No, seriously, whatcha got?"

John dipped his head. "Well, I was considering saying, 'I think she got the point.'"

"Ugh."

"Because, you know, I'll probably kill her with that spear, and—"

"Oh, I *got* it. I just didn't like it much."

"I thought if I cut her head off, I might say, 'That's *one* way to get a head in life.'"

"I guess I'll just have to hope you don't cut her head off, then."

They fell silent. There was a constant keening up here, a hot teakettle whistle. John's horse was jittery, and it was getting harder and harder to keep it in place.

"Where is she?" he whispered.

A crunching sound behind them answered his

question. He and Merle turned, expecting to see something vulture related, but the birds were gone. Instead, there was Saxbriton—bright eyed and pink, big as a whale, grinning like a bear trap with Merle's dead pony lodged between her jaws. She purred like a cat, tossed the limp carcass of the pony into the air, caught it square in her wet mouth, and swallowed it whole.

John's horse neighed and reared back—this was possibly not the battle-tested mare that she'd been made out to be. Saxbriton took a step up the mountain, and then another, blowing puffs of smoke and sucking them back again. Her slack wings splayed and unsplayed their fingers, the thumbs picking a path through the rocks.

"Um," said Merle.

"Here! Give me your hand!" said John as he reached down with his own. But Merle had gone stupid with fear.

The dragon inhaled deeply, and John thought he saw the gaps and seams between her belly scales flare suddenly blue.

"Merle! Now!"

Merle started. "What?"

"Give me your hand!"

Merle reached high, and with an adrenaline rush of strength John grabbed his wrist and heaved him atop his mount. Merle scrambled for handholds as John kicked the horse in the ribs and it carried them down into the

crater. There was a sucking of air, then a searing heat behind them as a blue jet of flame shot up the mountain. They half galloped, half slid down into the dragon's lair as her breath ignited the sky above them.

The ground shook.

Near the bottom of the bowl, the horse lost its footing and tumbled onto its side. John and Merle landed with a thump and a cloud of dust in the soft ashes. The horse righted itself and continued to bolt, and John and Merle could do nothing but watch it go as they rushed to hide themselves under the dark timber of the dragon's nest.

Saxbriton herself appeared at the top of the bowl, wings outstretched and taut, stepping lightly for something so large. She tracked the horse's movement as it clambered up the opposite side of the crater, and leaped after it. Her pink belly soared over Merle's and John's heads, tapering with the passage of her forked tail.

"See any weak spots?" whispered Merle.

"Not as such, no."

"Thanks . . . thanks back there. Lifting me up on the horse the way you did, that was amazing."

"Just don't make me do it twice," said John. "I might have dislocated my shoulder."

Neither Merle nor John could have guessed what a horse getting cooked and eaten by a dragon sounds like, but it turns out that when you hear it it's pretty obvious.

John had a pukey feeling in his mouth. "Where did the spear end up?" he asked.

It was lying a little ways off, half buried in ash. John went after it, moving slowly in his armor through the knee-high powder.

Then there was a rush of wind, and Saxbriton soared once again into view, her wings taking the air like a kite, her magnificent body steaming with heat and raw magic. Merle dug his little flashlight out of his pocket, switched it on, and chucked it in a hook shot over the top of the nest. Saxbriton chased it like a dog.

He'd bought John only moments, but it was enough for the knight to steady his lance and ready himself for another attack. But he'd expected the dragon to close in and snap at him with those teeth and talons, and now Saxbriton only pivoted away from the flashlight, propped her forelegs atop the pile of timber, and inhaled. Once again her belly glowed blue.

John dropped his spear and fell to his knees, crouching behind the chickadee shield as another surge of fire enveloped him.

CHAPTER 12

Soon the shield was too hot to hold, but the flames passed and John fell backward, gasping for air.

"She isn't running out of fire, Merle!"

But in truth she had, and Saxbriton advanced now, beating her vast wings and stirring up a storm of cinders and soot. John recovered his shield and grasped blindly for his spear, but it was Merle who got to it first, and the old man dug in and brandished it at the approaching dragon.

"Come and get it, you . . . marshmallow!" Merle shouted.

"That's telling her," creaked John.

Saxbriton swooped low, talons first. Then she wrenched the spear out of Merle's grasp and dropped it off the side of the mountain.

John was on his feet again, and both men stumbled

back to the cover of the nest as Saxbriton rounded back toward them. She screeched happily. They ducked and scrambled their way deeper into the pile of trees.

"Sorry I lost the spear," Merle whispered.

"That's all right. I was never sure what I was going to do with it anyway—apart from pointing it at her and hoping she ran into it."

Saxbriton screeched again, but there was a different tenor to it. Frustration. She didn't know where they were. The beat of her wings whipped the ashes and turned the crater into a dirty snow globe.

John coughed. "I'm tired, Merle." He sighed. "Already I'm so tired. My shoulder hurts and my . . . head feels funny."

John's head felt funny because Saxbriton had burned off two thirds of his hair, but now wasn't the time to mention it. "Let's get some of this leg armor off you," Merle said. "It's just weighing you down. No knight ever died of a leg wound." He tore off John's knee plates and went to work on the greaves. As he dismantled the armor, Saxbriton commenced to dismantling her nest.

She snatched up tree trunks in twos and threes and flung them to the edges of the crater. The woodpile shuddered ominously all around them. A scaly talon seized another trunk, this one dangerously close to Merle and John, and showered them with charcoal and twigs. But

Saxbriton still failed to spot them, and went to work on the other side of the nest.

"Okay," said John. "Now's when I have to attack."

Merle looked horrified. "Are you kidding? Now's when we run." He started feeling his way to the edge of the stack. "We gotta cut the line and let this one get away—she's too big."

John looked back and forth in consternation. Finally he chased after Merle.

"If I can't slay her now," he said, "then when?"

"You gotta stop thinking of yourself as the leading man all the time," Merle answered as he contorted himself through a gap in the logs. "That prophecy scroll the villagers showed us was a crock. It's some kind of Chosen One scam, to get out-of-towners to solve their dragon problem for them."

They reached the edge of the nest. Saxbriton was still picking at the other side.

"But I'm a knight," John insisted.

"And if we get the queen back home, everyone else'll be too," said Merle. He peered out at the crater's rise in front of him. "I know you want to be the one who does it, John, but you were never our only hope." And with that, Merle lumbered as fast as he could up the rocky bank.

John sighed and followed, and behind him Saxbriton squealed. John kept a hand on the hilt of his sword as he dashed up to the lip of the crater, caught a glimpse of Merle sliding down the mountain, then lost control of his own momentum and fell face first onto his breastplate.

He was skidding downward now on the loose shale, his armor grinding out a shower of sparks that bit at his eyes and face. He reached out blindly with his sword arm for something, anything he could use to halt his slide, and soon his hand closed over what he took to be a sapling growing out of the mountainside. It swung him around, and for a moment he was weightless. Then gravity reasserted itself, and he opened his eyes to find himself hanging off the edge of a cliff.

Legs dangling, he panted, "Merle! Merle?"

"Right here."

Merle was hanging beside him from another sapling. John looked up. No, not saplings—ribs. A blackened rib cage half buried in the earth.

"I already looked down," Merle told him between deep breaths. "Nothing good came of it."

John looked anyway. There would be a very long drop if they fell.

"Can't hold on," said Merle. "Can't hold on much longer. Too old."

"We're going to be fine," said John. He looked sadly at his shield. You couldn't see the chickadee anymore—it was black as coal. He was going to have to drop it if he was going to help Merle.

"Can't . . . even feel my fingers anymore," Merle added. "Tell everyone good-bye for me. Maybe . . ." He puffed. "Maybe you all can look in on my mom and dad. I'll be born soon. Maybe . . . you can all come to my bar mitzvah, say hi."

John dropped the chickadee shield and swung his left hand over to grasp Merle's wrist, just as the old man gave it up and let go. Merle dropped, then swayed beneath John as a freight train of pain traveled up the knight's left arm, through his shoulders, and up his right to the tips of his white-knuckled fingers. It was all he could do to keep from crying out.

Below them, something clanged.

"No!" Merle huffed. "Lemme go! You'll get yourself killed!"

Through the pain, John thought *it was the shield that had clanged. But too soon. It couldn't possibly have hit the ground so soon.* And just as he began to wonder where Saxbriton had gotten to, he felt a hot wind billow up from below.

The dragon was clinging to the mountainside, lightly, keeping her place with a gentle beat of her wings. She leered at them. She had a shield caught in her ear.

She's like a huge cat, thought John as Saxbriton's tail quivered. *She likes to play with her prey before she eats it.*

"Don't look down, Merle," he said.

"AAAAH!" said Merle, after looking down.

Saxbriton ascended, slowly, claw over claw, until she had only to stretch out her neck to bite Merle in half. The heat of her breath made them both slick with sweat, and John was considering whether a well-timed drop into the monster's mouth might get them lodged in her windpipe—they could choke her and all die together. *Better not try to explain this plan to Merle*, he thought as the dragon opened her jaws.

Then there was a burst of blue flame, and for a moment John thought Saxbriton had her fire back.

But it was Finchbriton.

The dragon shook herself loose from the cliff side and whined. The little finch held his jittery place in midair and let Saxbriton have another firecracker right in the eye.

It didn't appear to really hurt the dragon much— maybe she couldn't be hurt by finch fire any more than she could her own. But here was something new—a bright, fluttering thing—and like a cat, she went after it. In an instant John saw his chance, and let go. He and Merle dropped—not down to the rocks, nor into the monster's jaws, but square onto a frill of long scales that grew where Saxbriton's head met her neck. They slipped and flailed around for something to grab, or a foothold. Then they

held fast to the whiplashing neck as Saxbriton followed Finchbriton down the mountainside.

The little bird managed to stay just out of reach, even riding the blasts of air from Saxbriton's snapping jaws. *Now*, thought John, *would be a good time to stab this dragon with my sword*. But he could barely move his arms. He and Merle both were reduced to hugging the dragon's neck tight and blinking against the rushing air.

Farther down, around a craggy bend, Billy Butcher and William Baker were still astride their mules, looking at nothing. Billy chewed a bit of dried skin on his lip. William sniffed, then spat.

"Wonder how he's doin'," said Billy for what was the third time.

A little bird passed overhead. They craned their necks to watch it, then fell off their mules as it was followed by three hundred tons of pink dragon.

"Holy—" said Billy from his back in the dirt, and then he went to sleep for a while after a burned shield landed on his head.

William rolled over and watched the dragon recede into the distance. "It's heading straight for Reek," he said.

Finchbriton flew for the village wall and perched there. The village guards, seeing what followed, scrambled to ready their bows and arrows and pikes.

"THE DRAGON!" they called to one another, to

the people inside the walls. One man rang a stout bell. "MAKE FOR THE CELLARS! MAKE FOR THE CELLARS!" he shouted. "THE DRAGON COMES!"

Saxbriton reared, stretched her wings to drag the air, and landed just outside the wall.

"FIRE!" shouted the captain, and a volley of arrows dashed the sky. They snapped against the dragon's snout, were turned aside by her chest and even her thin wings, and broke against the frill of scales where John and Merle were hunched, shivering.

"Hey!" said Merle. "Hold your fire! Chosen One right here!"

The guards paused to listen, then started shooting arrows again.

Saxbriton shuddered, her belly went bright, and she spat a cone of fire against the village walls. Guards fled or fell. Finchbriton took to the air again, and the dragon whipped forth her neck, jaws wide, and when she shut her trap the finch was gone.

"FINCHBRITON!" John wailed, and for a shaky moment got to his feet, drew his sword, and plunged it two-handed into the back of the monster's neck.

Saxbriton roared, and the little bird flew out of her open mouth. The great pink neck drew back sharply, and both John and Merle tumbled to the ground.

"Oof," said Merle, and then he lay there, unmoving.

Saxbriton paced backward, swinging her head about. John stumbled and pivoted, avoiding her legs, and ran to Merle's side.

"Merle!"

"Whuh," said Merle. John took him by the straps of his backpack and dragged him clear.

More arrows came, but they were less than horseflies to the dragon. Now she saw John again, crouching over Merle, and she whined in confusion. Her eyes bulged, crescent pupils widening into full moons. She took a step back, then a step forward, and hissed when John turned to face her.

He swiped at the air with his sword. "Get back!" he shouted, and she did. She actually did.

He advanced on her, and she pulled her head back as she backpedaled. But John broke into a run and swung again at the nearest talon. His sword bit only superficially into a single clawed toe, but Saxbriton howled. She retreated farther, opened her wings, and took once more to the air.

"Is she leaving?" said a guard. "She's *leaving*."

Saxbriton rose and turned tail. She fled, not to her mountain, but over the eastern horizon.

"He turned her back," said someone on the wall. "HE TURNED HER *BACK!*"

"Merle," said John, returning to the old man's side.

"Did you see that?"

Merle was up on his elbows, squinting. "You mean when she turned into two dragons?"

"She was never two dragons, Merle. You have a concussion."

"She ran away," Merle slurred. "Both of her."

"Can you believe it?" asked John, rocking on his heels. "I barely nicked her!"

"But you scared her," Merle said. "You know . . . that may have been the first time she'd ever been hurt."

CHAPTER 13

The giant called Rudesby sat quietly in his underwear atop the flight of stairs.

He looked right through a narrow window into the bedroom of Fray the enchantress. But it was still dark, and there wasn't much to see. He leaned left and looked down at Tom-Tom, who was standing on the island rocks near the base of the stairs, watching him. It was Tom-Tom's job to make sure that Rudesby waited there for Fray to return.

He hadn't always been called Rudesby—it was just what the other giants named him. He hadn't even known he was a giant until he came here. Last night he'd dreamed that he couldn't remember his real name.

He might be dreaming right now. He often wondered if this could be true—certainly he'd had dreams before in which he was missing his clothes. But now, for the first time, he considered that he might be not dreaming, but dead. Maybe he'd died back in the canyon, and this was hell.

The faint noise of a door in the bedroom beside him snapped him from his thoughts. He bent his neck to look through the window and watched as motes of dust inside the room flared like matches and lit every inch of the chamber. Fray was done with her incantations and spell casting, he supposed. She threw off a thick shawl and crossed the room to open the thin window. Then she folded her arms on the sill and studied him.

"Hello, Rudesby," she said.

"'Lo. Done with your spell?" he asked. He knew everyone had trouble with his accent, so he spoke slowly, trying to imitate theirs. It made him sound like a halfwit.

"Quite so. The boat can find its own way from here on in."

She held his gaze for several seconds without speaking. But Rudesby had never had the stamina for long stretches of eye contact, so he looked away.

"They tell me you've been spending a lot of time by the west rift," Fray said. "Or should I say a lot of time by the tapestry? Perhaps you're just an art lover."

Rudesby shrugged. "Wanna go home."

"I know you do. And the invisible door by the tapestry does indeed go to your world, but it seems I need to clear some things up. For any of the doors to work, there must be another living thing on the other side to take your place. Nothing ever approaches the other side of the west door. And if by slim chance it did, and you were to cross over, you would find yourself in the most unwelcoming frozen desert."

"If . . . if nothing ever approaches, how d' you know what's on the other side?"

"Smart thinking. Some time ago I was fortunate enough to trade places with an unfamiliar kind of seabird. Nim was good enough to catch this bird and use it to bring me back. But you're too big for a seabird, Rudesby, do you understand?"

Rudesby looked at his fingers, poking each in turn as if he were doing math. "You have . . . three other doors."

"Indeed I do. And one, though it leads to the England of your world, is much too small. The next leads to the middle of an ocean. And the third . . . well, I think you already know all about the third. It brought you here. You could go back through it, and it would be as if you'd never come—you'd find yourself in thin air near a cliff, and high over a desert. Do you still want to die?"

Rudesby shook his head. "Don't wanna wear only underpants my whole life, either."

Fray smiled. "I'll talk to Nim about that. My giants are mostly boys, as you know, and boys do like their little clubhouse rules. But if you are going to be one of us, you ought to know our stories. May I tell you a story, Rudesby?"

The giant shrugged.

Fray began. "King Denzil XXXIII and Queen Rosevear had four sons: Fee, Fi, Fo, and Denzil. And the kingdom had great friends in the enchantress Lady Fray and her beautiful daughter, Princess Morenwyn.

"Pixie magic is rare, Rudesby—I don't suppose you know that. We pixies don't have the glamour of the Fay. But pixie magic, when you can find it, *confounds* glamour. The famous fairy luck tended to unravel. It's too simple a thing to say the fairies have good-luck magic and the pixies bad-luck magic, because one man's fortune is so often another's misfortune, you know, and vice versa. But if magic is a rainbow, Rudesby—and please forgive me for suggesting that it is—then the Fay glamour was ultraviolet, while a pixie jinx was pure infrared. Opposite ends of the spectrum.

"So I was always welcome at court with my pretty miracles. I enchanted their shields and made their swords sharper than they had any right to be.

"And we were all happy on our islands, away from the savage humans and inhospitable Fay. Morenwyn often stayed at court while I explored the world, and the sons of King Denzil made great fools of themselves to win her affections. You know how boys can be. Wrestling and sword fights and other nonsense—the sorts of things boys think will impress girls.

136

"On one day in particular I came home to the palace from one of my explorations, landing atop the castle walls astride a red-billed chough. I didn't wait for a proper escort, because . . . because I was a little too sure of myself back then. Instead I strutted down the center stairs and into Denzil Hall, promising some fresh entertainment.

"Instead I delivered a dreadful lecture—in my travels I'd discovered that the world was dying. In our isolation we'd failed to notice what the humans and elves already knew: that much of the earth had disappeared in a magical catastrophe generations ago, and that which remained? It diminished every year. The sky had not always smoldered in twilight—the sun had once been like to a ball of fire that crossed daily through the heavens, just as it was in our oldest stories. Of course the king and kingdom trusted their Lady Fray, and believed her?"

Rudesby flinched when he realized she was waiting for an answer. "No?"

"No. You may have noticed that people will take swift action to save themselves from immediate danger, but when faced with a creeping death they'll stand right in its path and debate its existence even as they're patiently trampled. In this regard the pixie people are 'only human,' an expression that most of them would find to be in exceedingly poor taste. So.

"Pixie scholars and courtiers filled Denzil Hall and

bickered and debated what to do about their waning world, and whether it was really waning at all. Throughout this I stayed at the fringes, frustrated but mum. I realize now that all the court could see that there was something I wasn't telling, and it riled them. 'Hasn't she always been a bit of an insufferable know-it-all?' they asked one another behind veils of hands. 'She with her secret magics and private jokes. Always laughing at nothing. Hers is a witch's laugh, have you noticed?'

"Before long the pixie kingdom was openly discussing the very real possibility of taking advice from the elves. Surely they knew more about this situation (if indeed it was a situation) than dear Fray?

"Now I broke my silence.

"'The . . . wise and learned court of King Denzil is joking, of course,' I said.

"'Lady Fray should take no offense,' cooed the arch

chamberlain. 'She has told us herself that her singular knowledge comes from traveling the wider world. The Fay—'

"I interrupted. 'The Fay have had nothing to say to the pixies for three hundred years, and likewise. You've not seen how they've changed. They've grown insular and weird. Tangled. They're bearing some bitter fruit in the court of Titania.'

"'Our dear Fray has confused the fairies with a patch of late October blackberries,' joked the minor domo. It was about as good a joke then as it is now.

"'The court of Titania has of late been nothing but civil,' said the minister of waves. 'A message of goodwill arrived from Her Majesty on feast day, borne by a most charming white crow. It promises a new age of friendship and sharing.'

"At this I raised my eyes. 'Sharing of land?'

"'Er . . . ,' said the minister. 'Possibly. The message said only 'knowledge.'

"I smirked. I was a great one for smirking. 'I'll bet it did,' I said. I'd backed myself against a wall, literally and figuratively. 'Don't make this mistake,' I pleaded. 'You haven't *seen* the fairies. You haven't seen how they bully the humans. They'll be bullying us next.'

"Murmurs rippled through the hall.

"The king stepped down from his dais. 'Surely Lady

139

Fray does not draw comparisons between the pixies and the *humans*.' It was very italic, the way he said 'humans.'

"I breathed, deeply and deliberately, and shared a look with my daughter, who was seated near the dais and surrounded as always by those idiot princes.

"'I haven't been entirely forthcoming,' I admitted. 'I have a plan. A plan to save us, and our children, and our grandchildren. I've been waiting to see if you all were ready to hear this plan. Maybe that was a mistake. But if the Fay are to be visiting . . . you'll want a clean house, naturally. Won't do to have an old black widow like me lurking in the corners, spinning webs. Daughter! Attend!'

"But Morenwyn wouldn't come.

"'We would prefer the lady Fray and her daughter remain,' said King Denzil. 'Guards?'

"Good pixie men, in arms and armor enchanted by my own magics, advanced like a drumroll.

"'Morenwyn!' I said. 'Quickly!'

"'I'm not coming, Mother,' Morenwyn said quietly. 'I'm to be married to one of Titania's changelings. To unite our peoples. It's been decided.'

"She'd said it so quietly that I couldn't hear her over the clattering press of guards. I'd have to ask about it later. For now there was nothing to do but cross my arms, tighten my tongue, and rattle a ticking string of consonants through my teeth. At this my body closed like an eye and disappeared. And if the spell went right, then the marble floor would have split and sprouted a soul-smelling bush that unfurled and spelled out dirty words with its branches."

The spell had gone right. The pixie guards backed away, waving the stench from their noses.

Queen Rosevear sighed. "Rude.

No one in the kingdom could have told you who was the first to refer to Fray as a witch, but the word stuck like it was her True Name, if pixies had such things. And the pixies heard nothing from her as the fairy delegations arrived on their shores, bearing gifts and asking all manner of questions, 'Where is your sorceress?' being chiefly among these. But no one knew the answer.

The elves assured the pixies that the world was as whole as ever. The changeling prince Dhanu himself claimed to have recently visited the frost giants of the

Americas, though he was reluctant to discuss any details of his time there. He courted lovely Morenwyn, and the two seemed to hit it off despite the height and age difference. The sons of Denzil privately lamented the loss of Morenwyn to an outsider, but they kept silent for the good of the kingdom.

So when Morenwyn disappeared in the night, none doubted that the witch Fray must have come and kidnapped her. They didn't know that Morenwyn had compared the changeling Dhanu to Prince Fi once too often, or that the couple had begun to quarrel, or that Dhanu, in a pique, had told her, "You can stay in this world and *die* with your Prince Fi then, for all that I care!"

So Morenwyn had crept from the castle, and found a seagull to fly her, and used her own feeble blood magics to find her mother.

"What was your plan?" asked Rudesby. "What didn't you tell your people?"

"That I had found an island—this island. That there were giants living on it, some of whom had come here from a distant place. That this island had invisible doors that might take us to a safer world. But I hadn't yet studied the doors, and I wasn't certain what we'd find on the other side. I thought it best to hold my tongue about them until I was certain, because I knew the Fay wanted such doors for wicked reasons.

"And then, one night while studying the doors, I fell into a trance. I had a vision of two worlds, split in twain by a stake or spear or sword. And a tear in the sky and a great void consuming all that is."

"That's the tapestry."

"Yes, that's the tapestry. I'm convinced now that the same instability that created the doors will one day tear the universe apart. But I don't know why. You can be a help to me, Rudesby, while I figure it out. Would you like to help me, Rudesby? Would you like to help save the universe?"

You could see the reflex answer, the first impression on his lips. "I wanna go home" is what he nearly said. But every boy, when he's young, secretly believes that someone will ask him to save the universe sooner or later. Rudesby was a man now, so for a moment he'd forgotten. He'd forgotten that when a princess or an old wizard or a race of friendly aliens or a pixie asks you if you'll help save the universe, the correct answer is *yes*.

Rudesby nodded his head.

"Good. Then I have a job for you. I had another vision a few nights ago, you see. I foresaw a familiar group of pixies, with two humans and a leprechaun. And they were determined to find their way back to our island. The boat I sent them should just be arriving. Be a dear and capture them?"

CHAPTER 14

"So that's it, huh?" Scott said as the boat neared Fray's island. "Her castle's bigger than I expected."

"I told you it was large," said Fi.

"Yesterday you called a walnut large."

"It was a large walnut."

"The dark castle loomed . . . ," Mick began tentatively. "The . . . great black castle loomed like a . . . a . . ."

Everyone held their breath politely, but Mick had stalled. He rapped his forehead with his knuckles.

"Juices aren't flowin' this mornin,'" he muttered. "It's all these pixies! My mind ain't in full flower. No offense, lads."

"The black castle loomed like a . . . big black tent," Polly offered. "Is that good?"

"The castle loomed like a *giant building* in the distance!" Fo announced.

"The trouble is that *nothin'* looms as hard as a castle," said Mick.

"The castle loomed like another, different castle," said Polly.

"The castle loomed in that fashion common to castles the *world* over," Denzil said with a flourish.

"Forget I brought it up."

"The castle loomed like a storm cloud," said Haskoll, "dark and heavy with portent."

"The castle loomed like a storm cloud," said Scott, "dark and heavy with portent."

"Hey."

Mick raised his head and smiled at Scott. "Well now, that's not half bad. How'd yeh think o' that?"

"It just came to me."

"Hey!"

"Brothers," said Fee. "Do my eyes play tricks, or is there a giant on the island's shore, awaiting our arrival?"

They all fell silent and looked. It wasn't a giant, of course—it was just a man, though Scott didn't feel like having that argument. A man in dingy underwear the color of a greasy napkin.

"They call him Rudesby," said Prince Fi, "and the last time I was here I gave him fair reason to have a grudge against me."

They couldn't have turned the boat around if they'd wanted to—a combination of tide and magic sent them hurtling toward Rudesby, grinding up the beach until they came to a stop by his feet.

"'Lo," said Rudesby. "I'm here t' capture you. It would mean a lot to me if you didn't make a big fuss about it."

Fee ran up the starboard edge of the boat to its prow. "You expect a prince of the kingdom of the pixies to come without a fight?"

Rudesby cringed. His whole *body* cringed. "Aw, man, I don't know . . . yes? Please?"

Up to this point, even Scott had been clenching his fists, ready for a scrap. But everyone kind of lost steam. Haskoll had disappeared again.

"I just . . . ," Rudesby whined. "It would be great if you guys would all be cool and just come along quietly, and then maybe Nim won't pull my ears and tell the others to call me Rudesby anymore."

"That's not your name?" asked Polly.

"My name's Chaz. Ha! Man, it feels good to say that. My name is *Chaz*."

Mick, who had been in a twelve-step program in the eighties, said, "Hi, Chaz" reflexively.

"My name is Chaz, and my life's been a big turd since Vegas, but if you let me tie up the kid and the leprechaun and stick the rest of you in this little cage here, maybe everything'll turn around for old Chaz."

The pixies huffed and grumbled about this, but Scott changed the subject.

"Vegas?" he said. "I *thought* you sounded American. You're from Las Vegas?"

"I'm from San Francisco," said Rudesby. "Me and my wife were on our honeymoon in Vegas, and after that we were gonna drive down and see the Grand Canyon. But I lost all our money at the tables and Lacey threw her wedding band at me and ran off with a magician."

For half a minute the only noise was of the dark waves lapping at the rocks and the *thunk* of the boat, rising and falling.

"Had just enough gas to drive down to the Grand Canyon by myself. Drove straight through the night. When I got there I went right for this thing called the Skywalk. It's awesome. It's this huge glass horseshoe that goes right out over the rim of the canyon. You can walk out and look straight down. It was Lacey that read up on it, Lacey that wanted to go see it, so . . . I guess maybe I thought she'd be there waiting for me. It was stupid."

Rudesby sat down on the rocks.

"So I didn't know I was gonna do it, but suddenly I'm jumping off the Skywalk, right? And I guess I go through some magic portal like in a movie, and I get caught in a net with all these eagles in this weird castle here. And it's just like in a movie, except in movies the main character doesn't get stripped down to his underwear and treated like a jerk, does he?"

"It's because you're not the main character," Polly told him. "I am."

"Oh. Hey. I thought all pixies were black."

"I'm not a pixie, I'm just magic."

"Look," said Scott. "We're not gonna let you tie us up or stick us in cages, but we'll come quietly with you if you take us to see Fray."

Fee and Fo raised their voices in protest.

"What?" said Scott. "We want to get inside and see Fray anyway, don't we?"

"Lad has a point," said Mick.

"We'll even walk . . . I don't know, single file or something. And you can bark orders at us."

Rudesby nodded his head—slowly at first, but with a rising vigor like he might just start shaking hands and passing out cigars, he'd never heard an idea so good.

"I think I'd *really* like that," he said.

"Okay then!" said Scott. "Um . . . everyone line up?"

"In what order, do you suppose?" said Denzil. "Oldest first?"

"How about biggest to smallest," Fee grumbled. "Everyone fall in behind Scott."

CHAPTER 15

Emily was in a dog carrier. The unicat was with her. Erno was in another carrier that she could not see somewhere behind her. They had called to each other, talked for a bit, made and unmade foolish plans. But in time it came clear that there was nothing to say, and now Emily was pretty sure Erno was asleep.

She didn't know where Biggs was. He hadn't returned any of their calls.

Emily had yet to hear about Scott's adventures in Pretannica—about the Tower of London that was enchanted to vanish with Queen Titania and all her retinue; about the huge ravens who felt its pull, compelled by the same spell to find it wherever it appeared. But she would have felt a kinship with those ravens now as she shivered in the cargo hold of a passenger jet winging its way over the Atlantic. She felt certain they were over the

Atlantic, because she began to feel a tug now—the pull, growing ever stronger, of home.

She couldn't say just how she felt it, or why, but Goodborough, New Jersey, was reeling her in with outstretched arms, a voice neither motherly nor in the strictest sense even human whispering, "Welcome back. We knew you'd be back. We kept your room just how you like it."

She surprised herself by getting a little sleep, too, the unicat curled up in the crook of her arm. She awoke when the plane touched down and went through the complicated business of remembering where she was. For a moment she even thought it might be that OTHER cage she'd been locked in, ha ha, life's funny, isn't it.

Soon a man came to take her cage off the aircraft, and she pleaded with him just as she had pleaded with the man who'd loaded her on board in London.

"PLEASE HELP ME! Please please please, I'm not a dog, I'm a kid! Please don't let her take me!"

"All right, calm down, calm down in there," the man told her as he wheeled her down a ramp. "Your owner's gonna get you real soon and it'll all be over."

Emily exhaled and hugged herself. The unicat licked her fingers.

Home was so close, now. She'd be in the Philadelphia airport, of course. Goodborough was across the Delaware River, just ten miles away.

She was taken to baggage claim, maybe the same baggage claim where she and the others had narrowly evaded capture by Nimue and her Freemen just a few scant weeks ago. She was wheeled up to a group of bags and saw, for a moment, Erno, through the door of his cage. Harvey was sitting on top of it—had he been on the flight too? He must have been. He must have been in the cargo hold, listening to the terrible things Erno and Emily said about him. Soon Emily's carrier was turned and parked neatly beside Erno's, so that she could see only slivers of him through the slots in the plastic.

"You okay?" Erno asked her.

She made a noise like a laugh. But not *exactly* like a laugh. She knew that her laughter had always sounded a little strange—to herself and to others—like it wasn't her first language.

"Am I okay? Even if I *were* still the smartest girl in the world I wouldn't know how to answer that question," she told him.

A teenage girl was crouching in front of their carriers and cooing at them.

"Who's a good dog?" she asked them.

"I'd treat that as a rhetorical quethtion," said Harvey.

"Neither of us is talking to *you*," said Erno.

"Aw, you're a yappy little fella, aren't you?" the girl asked Erno. This gave Emily an idea.

"Bark," she said.

"Bark bark," she said a second later.

"Hello, sweetie," the girl said. "Am I not paying enough attention to you?"

"Bark bark bark."

The girl looked at her strangely.

"Bark bark bark bark," said Emily.

"What are you doing?" asked Harvey.

"Hey, Mom!" the girl called toward the baggage carousel. "I think this dog is counting."

"Bark bark bark bark bark."

A couple other people had noticed this too, and now they crowded near the cages.

"Bark bark bark bark bark bark," said Emily.

"That's . . . amazing," said a man.

"Bark bark bark bark bark bark bark."

"STOP THAT!" said someone new, a man some distance away. "STOP THAT . . . THAT BARKING!"

The girl really stared inside the cage now, stared like she was trying to spot the differences between two pictures, which in a sense she was.

"There's a cat in there too," she said. "Why didn't I see that before? There's a cat in there with the dog. That . . . *is* a dog, isn't it?"

"Of course it's a dog," said a man who was breathing as if he'd run some distance to get there. "It's my cat and dog. Please step aside."

"*Sorry.*"

Emily pushed her face up against the door. This new man looked perfectly ordinary, but he wore a pink tie, so she assumed he was a Freeman.

Erno began barking "Jingle Bells."

"Stop that! Stop it!" shouted the man.

"That dog is barking 'Jingle Bells,'" said someone nearby.

"What kept you?" Harvey asked the Freeman.

The Freeman flinched. He clearly hadn't seen Harvey until just that moment.

"Oh. You're . . . Harvey, yes? I had the wrong terminal. *And* the flight was early."

"Thloppy," said Harvey. "Gonna hafta make the trains run on time if you wanna take over the world."

Emily took up "Jingle Bells" too, in unison with Erno. "STOP THAT!"

"What an awful man," said a passenger. "Talented dogs like that, and he doesn't even appreciate them."

"I don't . . . ," the teenager said. "I don't think those are dogs—"

"Of course they're dogs," said the Freeman. "Hello? Are you the person to talk to about signing for these animals?"

He grabbed a clipboard from an airline employee and

scribbled furiously over two forms.

"No, they're not," said the girl. "No, they're *not*. How could a dog count? And they . . . don't even look like—"

"Please get out of my way," said the Freeman, and he took up the handles of both carriers. Then they were moving.

Emily felt panicked. "You're right! We're not dogs, we're kids. Please help us!"

"That almost sounded like English," said the girl, following.

"Leave me alone!" shouted the Freeman.

"Hannah, leave that poor man alone," said a woman, presumably the girl's mother. "What are you doing?"

"I think I'm going crazy," the girl murmured.

Now Emily just felt bad. Not that she didn't continue to shout all the way out to the street, but it was no good.

"That was clever," said Harvey to the Freeman. "You have to admit."

They met another Freeman in a white van at the curb, and he helped the first one load both carriers into the back.

"You boys are thupposed to have thomething for me," said Harvey, before the van's cargo doors closed and Erno and Emily were in darkness again.

They didn't see what happened next—that Harvey was presented with another clipboard, an ordinary

clipboard that looked ridiculous under the curly scroll of parchment that was clipped on top. This parchment was meticulously illuminated with an illustrative border and flowing script, but it really just stated that Harvey was a free agent. As long as he took no action against Goodco, Goodco and its subsidiaries and affiliated organizations would take no action against him, in perpetuity, until the end of time. It was signed by Nimue herself, and beneath this Harvey countersigned his True Name. To the casual observer the document would have revealed only the most incomprehensible gibberish, punctuated at the bottom with the imprint of a rabbit's paw, but it was as legally binding as they come. It drew on an authority much older and more unshakable than the laws of men.

But neither Erno nor Emily saw this, locked up in the belly of the van.

"I'm having trouble thinking," said Emily in the dark. A second later she couldn't have told you if she'd said it out loud or not.

The van was moving. They were moving toward Goodborough. They were crossing the bridge, which Emily saw in her mind as a long white arm, leading to a flawless white face, a head. Goodborough *was* Nimue. It was Nimue's mind—she couldn't believe she'd never seen it before. The people of the town were only figments.

"There," said Emily. "We just entered Goodborough.

Just that second. Did you feel it?"

"Feel what?" asked Erno. "What do you mean?"

The road here had a loping rhythm, a series of bumps that thunked under each set of tires—*thunk thunk, thunk thunk, thunk thunk*. A heartbeat.

"I'm having trouble thinking," she said again. "I have the weirdest feeling that we never left Goodborough at all. That the whole deal with the cruise ship, and England . . . that was just a dream, wasn't it?"

"No," Erno told her. "No, we couldn't both have had the same dream."

Emily huffed, exasperated. "But we're not the dreamers, don't you see? We're the *dream*."

Erno didn't remark on this at all, which Emily took for agreement.

The van came to a final stop, the cab doors opened, two sets of footsteps rounded the van to the back.

The cargo doors yawned wide, flooding their eyes with light.

"She's waking *up*," Emily softly said. "I'm thinking having trouble."

CHAPTER 16

The humans of Pretannica had not quite invented the train.

They'd invented the steam engine, however, so the principle was there. There'd been some tinkering about with steam-powered cars, but no one had given any serious thought to laying tracks—laying *iron tracks*—all across the landscape. The Fay would have considered it to be outlandishly offensive, and the humans of Pretannica mostly did their best not to remind the Fay that they were there at all.

So what John and Merle and Finchbriton and the Queen of England were hurtling through the woods aboard at this very moment was more of an all-terrain steam rover. If you had to describe it succinctly, you might have called it a Victorian monster truck. That's what John had called it when it had rolled out of the blacksmith's shed.

Twelve feet high, it really looked more like a steamboat on wheels than an actual truck, with twin stacks of copper pipe belching a thick fog into the trees. Rubber had never been developed in Pretannica, so the tires were cushioned with woven strips of leather, and each tire could rock up and down with the terrain independent of the others, all behind a steel wedge like a cowcatcher that plowed smaller obstacles out of the way. It was still a jarring ride as the chassis rumbled over hills, stones, fallen trees, down gullies and up ravines.

Despite Declan Sage's protestations that John had agreed—*in writing*—to "slay" the dragon and not merely "superficially wound" it, John and Merle had still been greeted back in Reek as conquering heroes. No one had ever managed to hurt Saxbriton before (they were openly calling her Saxbriton now, as if there'd never been any doubt about it). Certainly no one had ever turned her away. The village was afire like a haystack of wild speculation— her wounds were small, but maybe she'd bleed to death of them anyway. Maybe she'd been so badly spooked she'd never show her face in Reek again.

The butcher and baker returned and even had John's chickadee shield with them, so this was briskly cleaned and the chickadee repainted by a local artist whose personal style looked remarkably like the ancient scroll they'd been shown earlier. They were offered fresh

clothes, yards of food and drink, marriage proposals. They seemed to think Merle would be more comfortable dressed in linen robes, and he was embarrassed to find that they were right. And all the while the Queen of England clucked her tongue and pretended to check the wristwatch she didn't have.

So when John and Merle had started making noises like "This garland of posies is very nice, but we really need to be getting up north" and "I think perhaps a more qualified person should baptize your baby, but while I have you here maybe you could tell me where we might get some horses?" eventually the blacksmith had disappeared and reappeared a few minutes later driving the Victorian monster truck.

"YES," Merle had said when he saw it.

"THAT," John had agreed, nodding.

The blacksmith was driving them now. When asked, he'd insisted that the truck didn't have a name, but as he handled the wheel he kept calling it Gwendolyn under his breath.

John wore a patchwork of his former armor, having found that it only weighed him down. So he had the breast and back plate, a gauntlet and sleeve for his sword hand, a pauldron for the opposite shoulder. Finchbriton sat on that shoulder, fluffing his feathers against the wind. Merle sat on the deck. The queen had been made comfortable in a small chaise bolted behind the steering column. Gwendolyn didn't have any kind of windshield, so they were all eating a lot of bugs.

In a few short hours they'd made it to a port in the northeast of Ireland. The blacksmith's brother knew a man who knew a man who had a ship that could take them to Fray's island. They looked up at this ship now, and the name that was painted across its stern.

"The *Titanic*," said John.

They stared at the stern for a moment, and when no one else spoke John went ahead and said it again.

"The *TITANIC*."

"It's just a funny coincidence," said Merle. "I refuse to dwell on it. What are the chances that *two* ships called *Titanic* could both—"

"Do NOT say it!" snapped the queen. "Have you not been paying attention? You are a man of science, Merle, so you might think that such careless words don't matter, but I am telling you that this whole *place* is pure story. This is where stories *come from*. Don't tease the bear, Merlin."

Merle grunted. It would turn out to be a moot point, anyway—the disaster that was coming wouldn't be coming by sea.

"This way," said the blacksmith, and he led them up the gangplank to meet his brother's friend's friend.

The *Titanic* was not quite like anything any of them had seen on Earth. It was a tall ship, three-masted, a galleon in a way. But this galleon had a wide paddlewheel in its rear and a stout steel chimney rising diagonally up from its poop deck. This chimney was greased just as John's armor had been, so the whole ship had a pleasant fish 'n' chips smell.

"Is this 'im, then?" asked a bearded, strong-browed dwarf with one arm. "Is this the Chickadee?"

John let out a long, slow breath.

"This is he," said the queen. "May I present Sir John."

John shook the captain's hand and glanced back at the queen. "It's Sir Reggie, actually," he said. "You knighted me under my stage name."

The captain was looking at the queen too, with narrowed eyes. "One o' the queens o' the Fay, is she? Never had a fairy on board before."

"I am no more fairy than you, Captain. I've been bewitched."

"Oh. Well. That's all right then—my apologies, mum. Any friend o' the Chickadee, an' all that. We'll be under way presently."

"Yours is a lovely vessel," the queen told the captain.

"Funny thing about the name, too," said Merle. "Where we're from, see, there's—"

"Merle!"

The trip, it turned out, was nothing but pleasant. The *Titanic* rocked lazily, the wind touched their faces, the masts creaked, and the gulls called to one another again and again, asking that question that all gulls ask but never answer. When an iceberg came into view, John was quick to point it out, but he needn't have bothered.

"What, that?" asked the captain. "That's always there. Some kind o' magical ice, that is. Never melts."

Merle went to the starboard railing and squinted at the iceberg. "Why would that be? What's the story?"

The captain shrugged, insomuch as a man with only one shoulder can shrug. It was like his whole body winked.

"Who knows? It's just one o' those things, innit? Why's the burial mound o' Armnwynn Amnydd only visible on Whitsunday? Why's the Black Tree o' Kilcormac black? An' why do eatin' its apples make your beard spell out the name of the girl you're gonna marry? Don't know, don't care. But when I finally meet a gal named Jenny Small, I'm gonna ask her if she wants t' see my boat." The captain waggled his eyebrows.

"Iceberg just appeared a few years back," said the first mate, a thin old man like a knotted rope. He looked as if he was going to say more, but whatever it was evaporated in the boozy haze that seemed to follow him around.

"I'm afraid what I am *not* seein' is this little island o' yours," said the captain. "I told your friend the black-smith, I told 'im, 'I haven't *never* seen an island like you're describin' in all my days,' but he asked me t' take yeh out all the same, what with yeh bein' the Chickadee an' all."

"Thought I saw an island in these waters once," said the first mate. He was rooted to one spot, swaying with the breeze while the crew hustled around him. "Years ago, a little black island. Thought I saw people livin' on it too, but never found it again."

John and Merle and the queen shared a look.

"I have an idea," said Merle, "but no one's gonna like it. I think we should aim this boat right for the iceberg."

"That's what I like about you Americans," said the queen. "Your can-do spirit. If a joke isn't funny, you just keep repeating it until it is."

"I'm serious," Merle said. "Captain? Would you be willing to loan us a rowboat?"

CHAPTER 17

Rudesby took Scott and the rest of them underground and then up a tall flight of rough stone stairs. For the sake of expediency, Scott carried Mick and his sister and all the pixies but Fee up the stairs in the backpack.

"This rucksack of Scott's needs a washing," said Fi. "It smells like a bachelor's apartment."

Mick clucked his tongue. "Man's entitled to kick off his shoes now an' then," he muttered.

The ghost of Haskoll was already at the top, peeking through the ceiling. "It's a big room, Scotty!" he called down. "With some real tiny ladies in it."

"Are these the same steps you climbed the last time you were here?" Polly asked Fi.

"Indeed."

"Did you?" asked Denzil. "I snuck in through a trap-door in the roof."

"I stood before the great window and announced my intention to rescue Morenwyn," Fo admitted sheepishly. "I was captured immediately."

"Captured like a gentleman?" asked Polly.

"I feel like I should shout at you to stop talking," said Rudesby.

"Well, go for it," said Mick. "Yeh gotta do what feels right."

"No talking!" said Rudesby. Then he glanced over his shoulder like he was looking for feedback.

"That was really good," said Scott.

They'd reached a metal grate in the ceiling. Rudesby lifted it up on a hinge. Haskoll, unbeknownst to all but Scott, popped up first.

"Through there," Rudesby said. "Um . . . NOW!"

"There yeh go, lad. Nice one."

Scott stepped up through the grate and found himself on the floor of Fray's hollow castle. Ahead of him, some twenty yards distant, was a tapestry depicting the end of the world. And in front of the tapestry, an enormous rift as tall as the castle. From the corner of his eyes, he caught sight of two other rifts—the tiny one that went to England, and another that connected to the ocean. He knew from Fi's stories that there was a fourth rift somewhere high above. Behind him was the magnificent window, a glittering jewel of glass and steel. Between the tapestry and the window was the golden monument, and Moren-wyn, and Fray.

"Hmm." Fray blew through her nose. "Not quite the helpless prisoners I was expecting."

"Pretty," Haskoll said of the monument. "Looks expensive. What is it, some kind of thing of some kind?"

Scott was surprised by how small the monument was, actually. He'd heard Fi's story, understood on some level that it was really only monumental to a pixie, but still he'd expected to be looking up at it. It was impressively shiny and jewel encrusted, but it was barely three feet tall.

Fi stood atop Scott's right shoulder and nodded at Morenwyn. She might have smiled.

"I count three princes. Where is the youngest?" asked Fray.

"Fee?" said Mick. "He's currently showin' your staircase what a dignified pixie he is."

Morenwyn was gliding forward, entranced.

"Daughter," said Fray, "do not approach—"

"Mother, look. A pixie girl—and yet not a pixie girl."

Polly waved. "I'm human! But I'm really small and I have wings, look!"

"She is our sister," said Fi.

Scott flinched his shoulders, surprised. Which meant that all of them were forced to flinch, really, whether they wanted to or not. "She is?"

"Well," said Fi. "In spirit, you know. I mean no disrespect."

"Oh, it's fine—I just hope you know what you're getting into, making her your sister. She always takes the last piece of *everything*, for starters."

"Do not."

"Yoo-hoo," said Fray, waving. "Scary witch here, remember?"

She had Scott's attention again, so he went down on one knee. "Lady Fray," he said.

"Whoa, now!" said Fo. "Why are you kneeling?"

Mick slid down from the backpack and kneeled too. Fi and Polly and Denzil joined them.

"I just want to make clear that I am *not* kneeling," said Fo. "I am *standing* on someone who is kneeling."

"Lady Fray, my name is Scott. I'm from the other world, the one where your portals lead."

Fray watched him, silently. He tried not to let himself get distracted by Haskoll, who'd floated up into the hollow tower above. "Oh, sweet!" he shouted. "Eagles!"

"I know that you think something terrible's going to happen, and it will destroy both our worlds," Scott told Fray. "I know you think it has something to do with the portals, and you're trying to figure out how to protect everyone."

"You flatter me, boy. At this point I want only to save Morenwyn and myself."

"You don't mean that," Morenwyn scolded.

"Some days I do. Oh, get up off your knees, all of you. Honestly."

Scott stood. "I just . . . look, I've figured it out. That you're responsible for holding this world together somehow. Is it a spell you cast, or—"

Morenwyn was smirking. Scott pressed on.

"—or is that gold thing some kind of magical antenna, or . . ."

He trailed off. Fray looked furious.

"I think you offended her," said Polly.

"Well, no one can say ych're not consistent," said Mick.

"Did I cast a *spell?*" said Fray. "What, a thousand years ago? By the Spirit, boy, how old do you think I *am?*"

"Whoopsie." Haskoll chuckled.

"The pixie people are not ageless like the Fay, Scott," Fi muttered. "We live the same span as do humans."

"Oh." Scott winced. "I didn't know."

"The largest thing I ever held together with magic is this castle, *boy,*" said Fray.

"I . . . I'm sorry, I didn't realize. I can't keep all this stuff straight."

"Did I *cast a spell*. You're as bad as King Denzil and his cronies. You think I'm some kind of genie—"

"Well, I'm sorry," Scott interrupted, "but I'm just really confused now! This island is the center of Pretannica!"

"Pretannica?"

"It's what we've been calling this world. Sorry. But if this world is just a bubble, then this island is dead center!"

Fray frowned. "Is it now."

"You didn't know?"

She huffed. "I've explored a lot of our world, boy, but I'm no cartographer. I don't have a map of the world's boundaries—"

"Well, I *do*," said Scott, and he rummaged through his backpack.

Fee poked his head up through the grate. "I'm here!" he panted. "I'm . . . what are we talking about?"

Scott slapped the Freeman's map down on the castle floor. "My friend Merle helped make the Gloria happen," Scott said, "with his time machines. It was an accident. But that was way over here, in Avalon. *Avalon* was the center of the Gloria. So why isn't Avalon the center of Pretannica?"

He thought he'd been doing pretty well but now saw that he'd lost Fray's attention entirely. She was looking past Scott at something out her window. Scott turned. There were a couple of figures, walking up the beach.

"More of your giants, Fray?" asked Denzil.

But they weren't. Scott squinted. He could just

recognize them—his dad, and Merle. Polly squealed, hopped up and down.

"My giants are in the caverns below for now," said Fray, "on my orders. But I'll confess it's not the figures on the beach that have my attention."

Scott saw it now too, a distant speck above his father's head.

"It's the figure in the sky."

CHAPTER 18

Emily was in a fishbowl.

That was how she would have described it later, if she'd ever described it later. A big round glass tank above a metal grate, and studded all over the top with retractable needles. At eight points there were holes in the tank for pink rubber gloves, pointing inward, that Freemen could use to maneuver Emily, or hold her still.

The needles connected to some kind of hospital diagnostic machine. The machine went *beep, beep, beep*.

She felt certain that Erno was in such a tank too. But she hadn't seen him since they'd arrived here, at the Goodco headquarters, on a man-made island in the middle of Lake Meer.

When the Freemen came again, she retreated into her thoughts. She didn't have to think about them pushing,

prodding, holding her with those pink gloves if she didn't want to. Instead she plucked at the wires of her headgear and recited pi to 116 places while a hypodermic filled with a familiar pink solution extended slowly toward her neck.

She didn't notice them leave.

Recently, in that ramshackle row house in London, she had broken Nimue's enchantment with a four-leaf clover, and it had been like the sun shining inside her mind. This felt more like all the windows frosting over. It dimmed the light, sure, but the frost made such *interesting* patterns. So intricate and interlocking, like a puzzle. She could stare at them all day. She did.

Suddenly, it became clear that this cage of hers had flaws. She could escape. It was so obvious.

She pushed one of the gloves inside out so that it was pointing away from her tank, and used the opening as a foothold. Stepping up, she snapped the longest needle off the end of its barrel and used this to perforate all the rubber seals that rooted the hypodermics in place. Before long she could rip out the seals and pull all the ends of the needles until she'd dragged that diagnostic machine right up to the tank.

The machine beeped, beeped, beeped.

She perforated the cuff of one of the gloves and ripped

it out too. Then she could reach through and remove the faceplate of the machine. With the front off, it beeped louder, as if offended.

It was a simple matter to change the waveform of the beeping to a steady tone, and then change the pitch of that tone. She was just going to have to guess at the resonant frequency of the glass tank, but she knew in her heart that she'd be right as she discharged the capacitors and the machine screamed loud, and high. She pulled her arms back quickly as the fishbowl shattered to pieces all around her.

She jumped clear of the glass and ran to the nearest door, then shrank as she heard approaching footsteps. The door opened before she could act, but it was no mere Freeman standing there.

"Dad!" Emily cried.

Mr. Wilson smiled down at her. He was dressed all in black, dressed for a rescue, and he lifted her high.

"Emily. Emily, I'm so, so sorry. I should have rescued you a long time ago."

"You were sick," Emily told him. "The Milk made you sick. You weren't yourself."

"Well." He smiled wider. "I am now. We have to move fast. I have a plan, but we're running out of time—Nimue's close to bringing Saxbriton across a rift to Earth."

"I know," said Emily, and she realized she *did* know. How curious.

Mr. Wilson shot a furtive glance around the corner, then carried her into the corridor.

"Erno's here too," Emily told him.

"I know. I found him first. He's safe."

"Biggs too."

Mr. Wilson checked around another corner, then turned down it at a run.

"I had a dream that you came to rescue me," Emily told him. She had to think about that for a second. "I've had a couple dreams like that, since they brought me here. But now it's *real*. It's really happening."

Something nearby was beeping. Faintly, but getting louder.

"What . . . what is that?" Emily asked. "Should we be worried about that?"

Mr. Wilson didn't answer.

"It's getting closer . . . or louder. The beeping. Don't you hear it? Dad?"

She looked up at his face, but the thing carrying her wasn't Mr. Wilson anymore.

She flinched and came to in the fishbowl. The cold glass cage with its gloves and needles intact, its beeping neighbor sitting unmolested across the linoleum floor.

A woman laughed, somewhere and everywhere—the forced laughter of someone who knows her joke isn't really all that funny.

CHAPTER 19

It was more than a speck in the sky now, and getting larger fast. As Scott watched, there was a flash of blue that quickly faded.

"I've only been on this rock a handful of years, Scott," said Fray. "I've been learning what I could about its doors. I've grown *sensitive* to them. If I concentrate very hard, I can even see the palest shadows of living things on the other side."

Scott was impressed. He could see the doors themselves, but he couldn't see *that*.

"I mention this," Fray continued, "because for all these years there has rarely been anything living near the western door, by the tapestry, apart from the occasional seabird. But for the last hour, there have been a great *many* living things by that door, and now something massive approaches. I can feel it pull, like gravity. And now . . . and now an altogether different *massive thing* descends on my island from the east. Do you see?"

Scott watched it get larger, this dusky pink, flashing thing in the sky.

"Boy . . . what have you idiots led to my doorstep?"

"Told you!" said Merle.

"So you did," said the queen.

"*Not* an iceberg," Merle continued. "Just some kind of illusion, to keep boats away from the island."

"Apparently."

John heaved at the rowboat and dragged it a little farther up on the rocks. There wasn't really anything to tie it to. He looked out at the *Titanic* and waved, though he doubted the crew could see them. It was pretty far away, and were they all invisible now because of the iceberg illusion? If everything went well with Fray, he wouldn't have the chance to ask them.

As he turned away from the ship, he saw it. The thing in the sky. The pink birdlike shape, the flash of blue as its jaws opened and closed.

"Oh no," he whispered.

"I SEEEEE YOU!" came a voice, impossibly loud, amplified as if by magic. Of course by magic. Only Morgan le Fay would cast a spell just to make her voice louder, because riding bareback on a fire-breathing dragon wasn't

terrifying enough. She sounded like she might still be mad about them rescuing Queen Elizabeth and then not dying afterward.

John scooped up the queen, quite possibly wounding her dignity in the process, and placed her safely inside his pack.

"Hell," said Merle. "Hell hell hell."

"You are my valiant knight," the queen told him from inside the backpack. "You faced her before, you can do it again."

"But it's worse than just a dragon, or just a sorceress," said John. "My ex-wife worked for Goodco. They sent her to Antarctica to investigate a really large rift down there. They knew it was there, they just couldn't figure out where it led to. It led to this island. I just showed them how to get Saxbriton to the real world."

"They're both real worlds," said Polly. "This one just has more special effects."

John turned. "Polly! Wh—? You're . . . how?" he stammered, his eyes popping at her size, her wings, the fact that she was here at all. "Ha?" he added vaguely.

Fi was here too, with his brothers. They all had new spears from Fray's armory.

John went down on his knees. "My little girl," he said. His hands hovered, aching to pick her up. "My surprisingly little girl. I'm afraid I'll break you. How are you here?"

"In recent times I was not entirely forthcoming with you, John," said Fi. "About our plans, I mean. It's a state of affairs that I hope to live long enough to rectify."

John tried to kiss Polly on the forehead, settled for kissing pretty much all her head and neck.

Polly winced, smiling and wiping her face. "Scott's here too," she said. "And Mick."

"They are?" said John. He looked desperately about for them as the monster in the sky barreled down.

"Finchbriton!" called Fi, and the finch descended and hopped across the rocks to where he stood. "Little bird, would you be my Pegasus?"

They whistled to each other, and Finchbriton took to the air above Fi, beating his wings in a hover until the prince could leap up to grasp one of his talons. Then they rose, heavily, into the wind.

"Polly, get inside the castle!" John shouted, just as Morgan and the dragon came into range. Morgan began raining down concussive blasts, as if they were her own furious thoughts given force and unleashed upon the island. Black rocks exploded and peppered the air. John ran out to meet Saxbriton, thinking he might draw Morgan's fire, and he caught the edge of a blast that sent him skidding across the jagged ground.

The dragon dove low and spewed like a volcano, spattering the island with hot bile and shooting a jet of blue flame through Fray's grand window. It shattered horribly, tragically, with a kind of Tinker Bell music that was entirely unsuited. Then Saxbriton pulled up, skimming the peak of the castle as she rose into the air. The course of her wings sent everyone sprawling, sent the pixie brothers' spears clattering back down to the ground.

"Polly! Merle! You both okay?" called John.

"Polly's here, she's okay," said Scott, who'd only just emerged from underground with Mick in tow. He was too large to have exited the castle at ground level as the pixies had.

"Scott! I wish you'd all just stay inside the castle."

"I don't think there's going to *be* an inside the castle soon," said Scott.

"I suppose you're right," said John, and he watched Saxbriton bank slowly and turn to strafe them again.

"Can anyone see Fi?" Polly called.

Fi, and Finchbriton, unnoticed by all, rose to meet the returning threat.

"I HATE YOU AAAALLLLLL!" Morgan wailed. "UGLY UGLY UGLY UGLY—"

It was anybody's guess where she was going with this—they'd never find out. She cut her thought short, having just spotted something small and unlikely in the sky ahead.

"SOME KIND OF LONG-LEGGED SPARROW,"

she murmured, her voice still unnaturally loud. Then the bottom half of this strange chimera—was it a pixie?—hurled a spear through her eye.

Her scream was a terrible thing to hear. It wasn't improved any when Finchbriton set her on fire, but they all got a break after she pitched off the dragon's back and fell into the sea.

"Ohmygosh," said Polly.

Saxbriton, on the other hand, continued heedless of Morgan's mishap. She skated over the top of the castle, just as Fray and Morenwyn appeared on the parapet. They shrieked and ducked, and the dragon raked a corner of the castle as she passed. The whole structure shuddered but held. John ran across her path as she snapped the air with her claws, and took a swipe at her belly before tumbling to avoid the crush. His sword bit deep, and Saxbriton cried out before beating her wings hard for open air again.

Merle was soon at John's side, limping. "I think she's still afraid of you," he said. "It's like she doesn't want to land."

"BRAAAAAAAAAAAHHH!" Morgan screamed, shooting like a rocket out of the ocean. Her head was all blackened like she'd gotten a face full of cartoon dynamite. There was a spear sticking out of her eye. She rose until she was several stories above the surface of the water, then hung there in the air, arms outstretched. Chanting. Fray chanted something of her own, and Morgan was beset by a hundred pecking seabirds.

"AAAHH!" said Morgan as she beat back keening flocks of seagulls. "DO IT, SAXBRITON! THE DOOR! DO IT NOW!"

Meanwhile the dragon had turned again, was reapproaching the island, and her belly glowed blue at the cracks in that familiar way. John looked around him—the island was scattered with people he loved, and it seemed impossible that not one of them would be consumed by the fire that was coming.

"Run!" he shouted. "Run *toward* her, not away! Scott, grab your sister!"

They did as he said, Merle, Scott, the pixies—Mick in Scott's backpack, the queen in John's. They ran frantically, recklessly, toward Saxbriton, and in a second the dragon stifled her fire—these insects were too close now to bake with a wide cone of flames. She'd hit one at best with her jet and waste the rest. Instead she threw her legs wide to slash at them with her claws, flicked her long tail to sweep them off the island.

John dove to avoid a front claw, rolled, hoped the queen was okay back there in his pack, and threw his sword arm high. It caught once more in Saxbriton's belly, held fast, and John was jerked from where he lay, carried along as the dragon hurtled toward the shattered window of Fray's castle. On the opposite side of the island, Merle was taken up by one of the beast's rough talons.

"Here," Scott told Polly. "Hold on to my jacket!"

"What?" she answered, but when he held her near it, she grabbed hold of his zipper all the same.

He ran, stuttering his feet, trying to time it right. Then he leaped, grabbed, and caught the spear tip of Saxbriton's devilish tail. He felt one of his shoulders pop. He would have liked to have asked Mick and Polly what they thought of the plan he was hatching—they were along for the ride, after all—but when the time came, all he could do was scream in pain, and that didn't explain anywhere near as much as he needed it to.

But he wondered: what happened when something tried to get through a rift and it had all these smaller living things holding on to it? What would happen if there weren't any other little living things on the other side of the rift with which to trade places? Would Saxbriton swap with the whale that Goodco was positioning anyway, leaving John and Merle and Scott and Mick and Polly and the queen behind? Or would all this added baggage prevent Saxbriton from making the Crossing?

That's what Scott was hoping for, anyway. He didn't count on a third possibility—that Saxbriton would cross, and that there would be enough Goodco people in place

on the other side for the rest of them to cross too. All of them but Polly, as it turned out.

The pixie princes were running alongside them.

"I can't hold on!" Polly squeaked.

"Drop and we will catch you!" shouted Denzil.

And she dropped. And they wouldn't have. But just then Fi, still holding fast to an exhausted Finchbriton, took her hand in his.

Saxbriton brought her wings in close, passed through the ruined window, and skidded to a halt on the opposite end of the castle.

Then there was that weird touchy-stomach sensation of being in a rift, and they were gone.

CHAPTER 20

Scott couldn't shake a kind of Pinocchio feeling—he had just, for a second, been in the middle of a whale. He wondered if the others had felt it. But now the whale was in Pretannica—in the middle of Fray's castle, Scott supposed—and he was home.

Home.

Home was cold.

It was cold and full of Freemen with guns, and it had a dragon in it.

At some point he'd let go of Saxbriton's wicked tail, and now he lay scraped and bruised on the Antarctic ice.

"Mick?" he said.

"Ugh," said Mick.

"Freeze!" said someone.

Scott squinted up at a man in a fat pink coat with a pink assault rifle. "Is he talking to us?"

"Couldn't be," said Mick. "I'm already freezin'."

"Shut up!" said the Freeman. "Shut up and don't move or I'll—"

WHUMP! A long pink tail sliced through the air and knocked the Freeman some sixty feet across the ice.

Scott scrambled to his feet and hustled himself and Mick out of the way. Saxbriton was putting on quite a show, whipping her neck and tail and beating her wings. She was surrounded on all sides by humans in pink coats, and she didn't seem to like it.

A lot of the Freemen were losing it. "The pink isn't working! It's like she doesn't know we're on her si—" one Freeman shouted, right before getting flattened under the dragon's foot.

A pair of tall mechanical cranes on tank treads flanked the rift—whale carriers, probably, connected by wide expanses of wet nylon netting. Saxbriton was stumbling through this netting over a slick patch of ice that looked to have been recently hosed down with fresh water. *Yes*, thought Scott, there were the hoses now, attached to pumper trucks—a ridiculous operation to keep a blue whale alive long enough to haul it across ten miles of ice. Some distance away Scott saw the ghost of Haskoll, pretending to ice-skate in and among the panicking Freemen. And a little beyond that, he spied his father and Merle and the queen, and he sighed with relief—even if they were currently being held at gunpoint.

Scott moved closer, trying to think of a way to help them. Saxbriton moved close as well, and one of the Freemen lost it—he turned, his allegiances forgotten, and fired off a dozen rounds at the dragon. It got the monster's attention, even if that was all it did. She snapped her neck straight and caught the gunman in her jaws, and most of the nearby Freemen scattered. Those who didn't got put to sleep with a sweep of Merle's wand. Others took shots at Saxbriton, short bursts of noise and light in this dim desert of ice.

"Do you think it's a coincidence that everyone we've met carrying a gun is superdumb?" asked Scott.

"Nah," Mick answered. "It's the gun that does it to 'em. Makes it hard to think about anythin' but the gun. 'S like carrying a load o' eggs—yeh can't relax till you've either set them down or thrown 'em at people, yeh know?"

"You're spending Easter with someone else."

"HOLD YOUR FIRE!" someone shouted. "WE HAVE TO CALM HER DOWN!"

But there was never any possibility of calming her down, Scott decided as he watched from a cracked shelf of ice. Nimue didn't care about her Freemen—she'd hardly need them after she raised her child army and brought her people through the rift. But she did need Saxbriton. She was probably calling out to the dragon right now.

As if he'd read Scott's mind, Mick said, "We gotta keep that dragon here, grounded."

Gunfire and screams echoed all around as Scott looked up at the nearest crane. "How hard do you think that thing is to figure out?" he said.

Saxbriton was fairly hopping about, pecking at Freemen like a hen.

"Well, she's officially off her diet," said John.

"Okay," said Merle, turning to the queen in John's backpack. "We're back on Earth. Quick—knight me."

The queen pursed her lips. "I can't knight an American, Merlin."

Merle blinked. He looked like he wanted to swear. "That's . . . frustrating."

"You should have thought of that before declaring independence."

John stripped off his backpack, and the queen fumbled to keep her balance.

"Merle, guard her. Or better yet, try to get her to McMurdo Station—that's an American base and it should be nearby."

"And you? What are you going to do, as if I didn't know."

John didn't answer as such. He just charged toward the dragon, sword unsheathed.

● ◐ ★

Scott sat in an uncomfortable chair in the crane operator's cab. They'd climbed atop this huge yellow two-headed tank of a thing, with its long skeletal arm saluting the sky. They'd found the driver's cab first, but that just made the tank move—and the tank *couldn't* move, not with its outrigger jacks anchoring it to the ice. Scott tried to make sense of the controls—he counted eight joysticks and sixteen buttons—as Mick read rapidly from the owner's manual.

"'The dragline consists of a bucket an' fairlead assembly,'" he said. "'The wire rope components are the drag cable, the bucket hoist, an' the dump.'"

"The dump," Scott repeated, nodding and looking with vague eyes at all the sticks and buttons. In front of him was a big pane of glass, through which he could see the Antarctic tundra, and what was happening there. He tried to pretend the glass was a television instead of a window. The television was currently playing a Japanese monster movie.

"'WARNING,'" Mick continued, and he gave Scott a stern look. "'Be sure the fairlead's in a vertical position when lowering the boom.'"

"The boom and the dump," Scott said. "Got it."

"Do yeh? If you don't have the fairlead vertical, you'll bend the boom base. Apparently."

"Which one's the fairlead?" Scott squeaked. "Which one's vertical?"

● ○ ★

John tried to get close to Saxbriton, but she was really worked up. She reared back, flashed her tail, batted at the ice with her talons like a cat. And soon she'd eat her fill and take to the air, and who knew what damage she'd do before they caught up to her again.

He ducked a claw and stumbled over the pink body of a Freeman. The Freeman's pink gun was right there. John had handled a lot of prop guns on the set of this movie or that—he knew how to work one. But he'd just watched a dozen Freemen bounce a thousand bullets off Saxbriton's iron hide.

Well, it wasn't any sillier than trying to stab her with a sword. He lifted the rifle and tried to track the dragon's head. No—not her head. Her *wings*.

"'The fairlead guides the drag cable onto the hoist drum,'" Mick quickly explained. "'The hoist wire is reeved through the boom point sheaves an' raises the bucket.'"

"Okay," said Scott. "You know what? In video games you can usually just pound every button really fast and still manage to beat the first couple of guys."

"I don't think Saxbriton is level one, lad."

But Scott was already doing it. The crane arm jerked, something clacked loudly that sounded like it shouldn't have, the whole contraption shuddered. There was a ball and hook connected to the giant arm with a metal rope, and this yanked on some thick nylon netting, which in turn yanked on one of Saxbriton's toes. So now they had her attention, and she wheeled around, went back on her hind legs, raised a front claw to strike. But then there was a *rat-a-tat* from below, and Scott's father was raking the dragon's wings with gunfire.

She shrieked as the taut sails of skin between her digits were perforated with holes. She beat these wings, rising slightly but listing clumsily to one side, and inhaled deeply until the barrel of her chest glowed like a Chinese lantern. John ducked behind his shield as Scott jabbed at joysticks, and the entire crane arm veered to the left. Which was directly away from Saxbriton, as it turned out.

"Other way!" shouted Mick.

But just as he was about to correct the crane's direction, Scott thought better of it; instead he pushed the joystick harder. The crane turned a full circle and clocked Saxbriton in the face just as she loosed her fire. The blue arc of it missed John, curved and engulfed the crane as Scott and Mick ducked, suddenly sweltering. They lifted their heads to find the windshield glass dripping from its frame.

"Nice one, lad!" said Mick. "Hit her again!"

Saxbriton tried once more to take to the air, just as one of the limp fire hoses suddenly sprang to life, whipping and thrashing and spewing water like an unwell anaconda. It soaked the dragon's belly, her back legs, her wings, and where the water landed it began immediately to freeze. Scott followed the line of the hose with his eyes and could just make out Merle and the queen crouching where it attached to the pumper truck.

"Merle!" John shouted. "I told you to get the queen out of here!" He was out of ammunition, and he hacked at the dragon with his sword. But it was dangerous work, and he never got a swing at anything more vital than a leg. For a moment it seemed as though he'd given up—when a claw came close he ran, then kept running in the direction of the other crane. Saxbriton watched him with interest, so Scott spun the arm of his own crane around again and gave her something else to think about. The arm itself whiffed, but the ball and hook at the end of its tether knocked her right above the eye.

"Did I hurt her?" Scott yelled. He tried to move the crane assembly away again as Saxbriton snapped at it.

"I think yeh're just cheesin' her off," said Mick. "Maybe if yeh were a knight?"

Saxbriton gave the crane arm a blow with her left foreleg, and now the whole thing bent like a busted antenna. The force of the strike clattered down the arm into the cab and rattled Scott's teeth.

"I'm the son of a knight!" he said. "What does that make me?"

"A knot," said Haskoll. He was suddenly there in the cab. "Get it? NOT a knight? Wordplay."

By now John had scaled the other crane, shinnied up its arm, and looked to be about to do something heroic and crazy. Scott kept his own crane moving so the dragon wouldn't notice John leaping off the other and onto her back.

He landed with an "Oof!" that carried weirdly across the flat ice, and plunged his sword into Saxbriton's shoulder, just between her leg and wing. She screeched, her neck whiplashing about, a contrail of blue smoke pouring out the side of her mouth.

Scott twirled the crane arm around again, and when Saxbriton snapped at the end of it, the ball and hook lodged inside her mouth. Scott tugged, but the dragon tugged back. The dragon was stronger.

"Give her a little line, lad!" said Mick. "You got her! Look how she slips! She can't keep her balance on all that fresh ice."

The crane whirred, its gears grinding.

"*Fresh ice,*" Scott whispered.

"What's that, lad?"

"It was my rap name back in high school," said Haskoll. "Fresh Ice. I'm flattered you know that, Scotty—you find a copy of my old yearbook or something?"

Scott ignored him. "I'm just remembering something

200

from my mom's emails," he told Mick. "This part of Antarctica isn't even land. It's just a layer of ice, and then ocean below that."

"Yeah?"

"Is that true?" said Haskoll. "Hold on."

The ghost dove through the floor of the cab, through the treads of the crane, through, presumably, the ice below.

John tried to get into a crouch in the crook of Saxbriton's wing shoulder, a tricky proposition even if the frenzied dragon weren't slick with ice. He hacked once at that wing, lost his balance, and bounded awkwardly— he flew from the creature, barely grasped the end of the crane's hook and tether on the way down, and swung a low arc before he lost his grip and slid several yards over the ice.

John didn't get up, not immediately. Scott focused on the dragon. "If it's just ocean under there, and we could somehow get her to breathe fire straight down . . ."

Mick nodded. "Yeah. That's thinkin'. I'll go get word to your da."

Just then Saxbriton gave a spirited tug, and the whole crane leaned. Scott had the sensation of that endless second between realizing that you've tipped backward too far in your chair and the actual moment you embarrass yourself in class. The crane toppled, and Scott clutched tightly to his seat as the whole thing came down on its side with a powerful thud. He looked for Mick, but the leprechaun had jumped free and was already halfway to John, who was just getting to his feet.

Haskoll reemerged, now perpendicular to Scott. "It's totally true! Just water down there!"

"I know it's tru—"

Then the crane's arm jerked again, and the machine was dragged a foot. The hook was still in Saxbriton's mouth, maybe even lodged down her gullet. The crane dragged some more, and Scott leaped through the open windshield and hit the ice running. Running, then slipping, then drifting to a halt with a turned ankle.

"Ow."

He was breathing hard, the Antarctic air scoring his lungs. Haskoll stood above him, offering a hand.

Scott took it and started to rise, but the ghost's grip was all cobwebs and dust. He fell backward again on his tailbone.

"Ow."

"Sorry, buddy. Guess you're not magic enough."

Saxbriton finally bit off the metal cable and swallowed the ball and hook. Now John had her full attention again. Scott could see him fifty yards away, straining to listen to something Mick was shouting into the bitter wind.

Then he saw his father straighten and face the dragon.

Saxbriton's belly went blue again, then white-hot, as she prepared to roast the only human here who mattered, the only one she was really afraid of.

John began to sprint across the ice, to sprint *toward* her, but that trick wasn't going to work twice. The knight wouldn't be fast enough. Scott held his breath, but the dragon didn't. He could see the searing ball of it climb the length of her neck to her throat.

Then John brandished the chickadee shield in front of him, two-handed, and jumped. He scooped the shield beneath him and landed atop it, on his knees, riding it like a sled across the slick wet patch of ice between Saxbriton's legs.

She followed his progress with her eyes, let loose her blue flame, but the knight was faster than expected. She cut a fiery path behind him, between her own talons, beneath her and on past her own tail. John's shield caromed off a back leg, and he wiped out but continued to skid on his own breastplate, the flames licking behind him.

There was a crack like a rifle, but it wasn't a rifle.

Merle had some small control over the fire hose, which is to say that he had as much control over the hose as the hose had over him. But he was able to keep the spray of it on the dragon as another thundering crack echoed through the ice.

Saxbriton had melted a bowl beneath her, and now the bottom of this bowl gave out. The dragon plunged into the cold water as the ice cracked and calved all around.

John staggered to his feet and began to run. The ground came apart beneath him. Merle and the queen ran too, just as the pumper truck tilted and skidded toward Saxbriton's monstrous, flailing body.

She howled, threshing her tattered wings—but these were stiff, numb, and heavy with ice. She could barely keep her head and chest above water. Her struggles made a frigid fountain that surged over one icy bank, then the other.

John approached, carefully. Saxbriton tried to light her fire again, but it was too soon, or she was too cold. She got her forelegs over the shelf of ice, and when this crumbled she did it again. That's where John met her, his sword arm level with her wavering chest.

He stabbed her through the heart.

She sank, still fighting, her hot blood boiling the water around her. Her chest disappeared, and her legs; her long neck snaked beneath the ice, then her nostrils, then bubbles and nothing. After she was gone, John stood and stared at the hole for a long time. He was still doing it when the others joined him—Merle and the queen and Mick and Scott.

"You did it," said Scott, because he felt like somebody should say something.

"I know. I know what I did."

They stared at the hole. In another moment they were going to feel the cold again.

"They're never monsters right at the end," John added. "Have you noticed?"

CHAPTER 21

Emily had just been rescued for the fifth or sixth time by Mr. Wilson when she came back to the fishbowl again and heard a noise. Not laughter this time, but a keening. A wailing *no*.

Emily didn't have it in her anymore to smile. But Nimue was screaming, and that was something. Saxbriton was dead.

The door across the room—the door through which Mr. Wilson kept appearing—opened now. It wasn't Mr. Wilson who walked through this time, though.

"This changes *nothing*," said Nimue as she strode, or glided, up to the cage. "Do you hear me? Can you still understand, darling? Nothing. I do not need Saxbriton to win."

Emily had no idea if the Fay woman standing before her was real or not. In Nimue's case, she wasn't certain it really made a difference.

"Maybe you *don't* need Saxbriton," Emily agreed. "But no dragon *and* less glamour *and* a smaller child army because of all that Milk-Seven we destroyed? I wonder."

Nimue stared. Her gown writhed. Her hair threw black fits around her head and neck.

"Had any visitors since you arrived, dear?" she asked, counterfeiting a smile. "Any friends or family?"

"Mr. Wilson's stopped by a few times. He said to say hi. Where's Erno?"

"In another needle room, somewhere," Nimue answered with a vague wave. "His mind isn't as welcoming as yours, so I've given him something to read. A little family history, you could say."

"Scott and John and everyone will stop you," Emily said. It sounded stupid, even to her.

Nimue mastered herself, and her hair and clothes were still. She looked calm, even sad. "Oh, Emily," she said. "Why do you hate my people?"

Emily started. She looked the Lady of the Lake in the eyes, and didn't have a ready answer.

"I . . . can't see them now, you know," Nimue added, though she wasn't really looking at Emily anymore. "We have a giant in chains on the sixth floor, and we've taken all his glamour, and now I can't see him. The Freemen with their pink lenses tell me he's still there . . . but."

She touched at her own face, as if feeling for cracks.

"Isn't that odd? I have glamour to spare, but I still can't see him. I wonder why that is," she said with a look that told you that she knew exactly why that was. Her eyes met Emily's again.

"Someone had to be the serpent in this story," she said.

The door behind Nimue opened once more, and now a murder of crows entered—eight Freemen in black robes, each wheeling some piece of weird equipment ahead of them. They arranged these pieces in a circle and began fitting them together.

"You're starting it," Emily said. "You're starting it now."

"You thought I'd wait for Beltane, for May Day? Well, so did I. But I seem suddenly to have a deadline I didn't anticipate. You can think on that, when it's done—that you and your friends succeeded only in bringing about the end of your world that much sooner."

The Freemen were constructing an octagonal pavilion, studded all over with jittering golden batteries.

"I'm kidding, of course," said Nimue. "I'll be doing all your thinking for you from now on."

With this she turned, her dress spinning, and let her Freemen build a magical power station around her.

Each of its eight sides thrummed with stolen glamour, glamour from Mick and Harvey and a litany of other poor unfortunates. Each of its sides was tethered to a thick electrical cord, and these were gathered into a bundle that spooled away from the octagon to a dynamo near Emily's fishbowl.

The black-robed Freeman who joined the power cords to the dynamo then approached Emily, head lowered, and kneeled just outside the glass of her cage. His head lifted and his eyes met hers.

It was Mr. Wilson. Of course it was Mr. Wilson. Nearly everyone she'd met today was Mr. Wilson.

"Dad," said Emily. "Woohoo. You're here to save me."

"No," said Mr. Wilson. "No, no one is coming to save you, Emily. You're going to die here."

Emily frowned and shrank to the back of the fishbowl. "Well this is different," she said.

Mr. Wilson crouched low and leered up at her from the floor. His teeth were crooked, his face dirty.

"You think you deserve to be rescued?" he said. "Do you?" A cough rattled his body. "Do you?"

"Is this a rhetorical ques—"

"After what you've done? After you left two goblins to die burning in that London deathtrap? Chained them with cold iron, didn't you—but it wasn't cold for long. *Was* it?"

"Um—"

"Their bodies ruined, burned to cinders, but it takes a stronger fire than that to burn away the magic, Emily. It

210

takes more than a bonfire to kill a goblin—"

Even if he *had* let Emily get in a word, she probably wouldn't have warned him about the second hooded Freeman sneaking up behind him. This second Freeman raised a shining monkey wrench and brought it swiftly down on the back of Mr. Wilson's head, and with a ripping sound Mr. Wilson's robes and body scattered like dry ashes to reveal two blackened little goblins underneath.

"Naked!" said the one on top before tumbling to the floor. "Naked again!"

"Your fault, Mr. Poke," rasped the other. "The head of the donkey was improperly made."

"The ass of the ass is an ass," answered the first, and they both ran off into the darkness, shouting the kind of language that would have made an ancient Celt blush, had there been any ancient Celts hanging around.

The second Freeman glanced over his shoulder at the others, and at Nimue—but they were still occupied with their improbable machine. He removed his hood.

"Hello, Emily," said Mr. Wilson with an empty smile. He had a red welt on his forehead and one of his lenses was cracked.

"Ohhhkay." Emily sighed. "Now we're back on track."

"We have to hurry," he said. "While Nimue and the rest are distracted."

"Quality plan, Dad."

He punched something into a keypad that Emily couldn't see, and the walls of the fishbowl rose just a little above its floor, just enough that Emily could slip through the gap. But she didn't slip through the gap.

"Quickly," said Mr. Wilson. "Don't be afraid."

Emily rolled her eyes and pushed herself off the base of her cage and onto the floor with a minimum of effort. Mr. Wilson's hand darted inside his robe and reemerged with a corn-husk doll as big as Emily, wearing the same hospital gown. He slid it inside the cage and closed everything up again.

"What is that?" Emily asked him, though she had a guess.

"Decoy."

He took her hand and away they ran, through the dark to a red-lit door in the far corner.

"I have a theory?" said Mr. Wilson. "That the entire Goodco headquarters—that the island, even—is imaginary. It only exists because everyone in Goodborough believes it exists. I've been circulating an email saying it's a hoax, that it's just a big painting in the distance. If enough people believe me, we should be able to walk out through the walls."

"Uh-huh. And that big red mark on your forehead?"

Mr. Wilson adjusted his cracked glasses. "It didn't

work on the way in."

Nimue's voice buzzed suddenly, like a hornet in Emily's mind.

Where are you going, dear?

They pushed through another door, and there was another fishbowl, and Erno.

"Emily! Dad!" he shouted. He threw down a file folder filled with pages and pressed his face against the glass. "All right!"

Mr. Wilson entered his code, and now Erno was free too. He hugged Emily. She stood in the center of the hug like a void, like the hole in a doughnut.

"Where am I going?" Emily muttered. "You tell me. This is your dream."

Not this time.

Erno drew back. "Did you say something?"

Emily tried to take stock of all her senses. The warmth of Erno's body. The dizziness, the harsh lights of the labs, the smell of chlorine and frosted corn. It seemed real, but it had always seemed real.

Mr. Wilson was sniffing around. Actually sniffing. Emily could feel Erno's eyes on her as he said, "Nimue gave me my file. To read. Mr. . . . Mr. Wilson?"

The frazzled man turned and looked at Erno, or at least in the boy's direction. There was something unfocused about his gaze, like he was trying to watch two television channels at the same time.

Erno had a question for Mr. Wilson. It appeared to be a hot potato, this question.

"You're . . . you're my real dad, right?" Erno asked, pantomiming a shrug. "My . . . biological dad."

Mr. Wilson seemed to be really thinking. He searched the air around Erno for some clue, then once again flashed that empty smile.

"I used to know this," he said.

"Yeah." Erno shrugged again. "Never mind. I guess it doesn't really matter anyway."

Mr. Wilson stared for another few beats. "Better go," he said.

He began dragging them both through another flashing corridor. "Now," he said, "we just have to find—"

A door at the end of the hallway leaped off its hinges with a screech, hit the opposite wall with a clang.

"Mr. Biggs."

A giant filled the corridor—still wearing the button-up pajamas that had recently been the only protector of his modesty, but which were now getting a lot of assistance from the six-inch-long chestnut-brown hair that covered every square inch of his body.

Gunfire crackled behind him. He rushed toward them—first running, then galloping like an ape—

"YAA!" said Mr. Wilson.

—then took them in his arms and vaulted up through the pressboard ceiling.

Erno's voice carried through the darkness, muffled where his face pressed against Emily's shoulder. "Wait! The cat," he said. "What about the unicat?"

No one answered. Biggs's fur was soft, his breathing even. All was confusing in the dark crawl space between the floors, but Emily was watching two channels at once too—part of her mind was still in the room with her fishbowl, watching the anxious Freemen through Nimue's eyes. The golden batteries of the magical machine spun around her. The Lady of the Lake must have been glowing like a candle.

"If this isn't one of your head games," Emily whispered, "then why didn't you try to stop me?"

Stop you? came Nimue's lustrous voice. *Precious girl, you're my greatest creation. My horseman. Why wouldn't I want you loosed upon the world?*

Emily winced, and breathed. "Well . . . call off your flying monkeys, then," she said. "Your greatest creation is about to get shot in the back."

They crashed down through another part of the ceiling, and Biggs carried them through a door to a stairwell at the end. Shouts followed them, then the crack of another gun.

● ○ ★

Inside the octagon, Nimue's hair danced, the hems of her gown floated implausibly around her.

Biggs had put them down, and they were running through a vast cold room where a flickering giant tugged listlessly at the shackles that chained him to the wall.

The batteries circling Nimue flickered too—golden, then pure white, and the Freemen backed away, shielding their eyes.

Biggs shielded their bodies—Emily's, and Erno's, and Mr. Wilson's—on the roof of the headquarters while a dozen men with rifles told them it was over. Erno insinuated that now might be a good time for Emily to accidentally turn the Freemen into mushrooms, or toads, or lightning bugs.

And the batteries were mere lightning bugs, while Nimue was the lightning—Nimue at the center of a tantrum of fire and possibility.

Biggs gathered them up once again in his impossible arms, and then his impossible feet swept them to the edge of the roof and he stepped out onto nothing at all—
    —weightless—

—weightless—

—and now Nimue was becoming something more, becoming the *Godmother*—

—and Emily, Emily was becoming something decidedly less.

CHAPTER 22

Scott and the others radioed to the American Antarctic base and were picked up by a big red-and-white vehicle with stout black all-weather tires called a Terra Bus. Called, specifically, IVAN THE TERRA BUS, if the sign painted on the side was to be believed.

The bus was *slow*. They bounced in their seats, fidgeted, their hearts straining against their chests. Here they needed a speeding motorcade, and the only available transportation was a cartoon tortoise.

"So," Mick said with a gleam, scootching up onto the bench where the tiny Elizabeth II was sitting. "Is there a *mister* Queen of England?"

The queen shifted slightly away. "Certainly there is," she said primly. But a moment later she was smiling out the window.

McMurdo Station wasn't as Scott expected—he'd

been looking out the windows of the Terra Bus for a single snow-buried building, but the base was more like a small town. There were dozens of buildings, places to eat, two bars, even gift shops. Something like a thousand people lived here. There was soft-serve ice cream in the cafeteria.

They used phones on the base to call Erno and Emily, but their mobile numbers just rang and rang.

The staff at McMurdo Station was introduced to the Queen of England, and then things really got rolling. She explained to them roughly what had brought her here, and of the great calamity that was befalling the world. She demanded immediate transport off Antarctica and was promised it without question. Oddly, the fact that she was two feet tall only made everyone listen to her more. Clearly this was a woman who knew things the rest of the world didn't.

There were already reports of trouble back home—thousands of children suddenly missing, or found wandering the streets, all walking in the same crooked direction. Children blank-faced and empty of affect until you got in their way, and then they fought you tooth and nail like animals. And not just children—adults too. There were two adults here, at McMurdo Station, who'd sleepwalked right up to the edge of the sea, trembling in their sleep clothes. One of them was possibly going to lose some toes to frostbite.

"I don't know where they thought they were heading," the station manager told them.

"New Jersey," said Scott.

The manager frowned. "Why New Jersey?"

Merle shook his head and said, "There's never been a decent answer to that question."

Military planes came to the continent from time to time, bringing new people and supplies, taking researchers home again. There wasn't a flight scheduled to leave anytime soon, but exceptions could be made for medical emergencies, and the Queen of England being only two feet tall seemed like as much of a medical emergency as anything. Soon they were winging their way to New Zealand on a gray, no-frills passenger plane.

Scott sat with Mick, his insides dissolving with worry.

"I lost Polly," he said.

Mick nodded. "I lost Finchbriton. Don't yeh fret—they all have each other. An' a pixie-girl can make the Crossing easier than most."

Scott looked over his seat at John. "I lost Polly," he said.

"I know," said John. "You did all you could."

"I just . . . lost her."

"We'll get her back."

They landed in a city called Christchurch, where a Royal New Zealand Air Force Boeing jet was waiting to take them to Los Angeles, then New Jersey. Aboard this new plane, the queen established a video link to the office of her prime minister in London.

He stood, surrounded by staff, and bowed his head quickly, as if afraid to take his eyes off the screen. He had the uncertain look of a man who suspects he's being pranked. Who knows the boutonniere is going to squirt him in the face but whose position requires he smell it anyway.

"Your Majesty," he said. It sounded a little like a question.

"Prime Minister," said the queen. "I bring alarming news."

"Yes? I mean . . . do you?"

"The world is in peril, Prime Minister."

"Ah. Bad luck, that."

"The woman you've called queen these past months has been an impostor. I am Elizabeth Alexandra Mary Windsor and I was kidnapped, but I am once again in safe hands. On a Kiwi Air Force jet to the States, specifically. I suppose you're not going to believe me now."

"Um," said the prime minister. He looked over his shoulder at some aide, and then back at the screen again. "Thing is, we might, actually. We've been keeping it quiet, but when the queen didn't rise at her usual time this morning, one of the house staff checked on her and found her skin to be . . . ah . . . *empty.*"

"Then there are two goblins on the loose, possibly still in the palace. We will have to have it fumigated."

"Your Majesty . . . I ask this merely in the spirit of scientific curiosity, but . . . are you—?"

"Currently two feet tall?" said the queen. "I am. I congratulate you on your keen powers of observation, Prime Minister. I assure you I feel otherwise fine. Better than fine—though I am short in stature, I seem to have all the strength of my customary nine stone. It's quite invigorating."

Scott unbuckled, and he and Mick moved to empty seats behind John and Merle so that they wouldn't disturb the queen.

"Yeh seem upset," Mick told him.

"I *am* upset."

"What about?"

Scott gave him a look.

"All right," Mick admitted, "but what particularly?"

Scott chewed a nail. "Erno and Emily and Biggs. I called each of their phones six times from the base."

Mick nodded. "In hidin', I expect. They might've ditched the phones too," he added. "Like in case Goodco could track 'em? Stop me if I'm embarrassin' myself—technology isn't really my breadbasket."

"Aw, you'd never know it, Tiny Tim."

Scott sighed. "Oh good," he muttered. "Haskoll's here."

"What's that, lad?"

The ghost had popped up in the row behind them. Scott hadn't seen him in a while and had begun to hope that he'd moved on to his great reward or whatever.

"Nothing," said Scott. Then he screwed up his face. "No, you know what? It's not nothing. The ghost of Haskoll has been following us around for days, and I'm the only one who can see him, and I'm sick of pretending otherwise."

"Well, that just sounds like crazy talk, Scotto."

Mick looked like he might feel the same way. "Haskoll . . . that's the changeling, tried to kill yeh last year? Harvey dropped a plane on 'im?"

"Not how I would have put it personally—"

"It doesn't matter," said Scott. "I don't want to talk about him. I want to talk about this whole question of the circles."

"What's this?" Merle asked, twisting to look back at them.

"Emily says the Gloria and the worlds separating was because of what happened in Avalon, when you and Arthur activated your time machines."

"Plus something else," Merle reminded them. He had a pleading look. "She said something else was at fault— some kind of big, magical hoo-ha."

"Okay, sure. But the point is, if it started in Avalon, then why isn't Avalon the center of Pretannica? Instead the center is Fray's island, but Fray didn't seem to know anything about that."

"She's lying."

"Maybe. I don't think so. Did you see that golden monument of hers?"

"No," Merle said. "I mean, Fi mentioned it, but when we tore through Fray's castle I was too busy trying not to die to really notice anything else."

"Fi also said the monument was Fay magic, not pixie," Mick added. "I'd have to agree."

"This scene is boring," said Haskoll.

Scott pictured the golden monument, tried to remember the whole scene. Tried to get hold of this strange feeling he had that it should be reminding him of something. The gleaming shaft of the monument in the middle, the tall window on one end, the tapestry on the other. The tapestry with that now-familiar symbol of two worlds split by a spear or sword . . .

Some movement up front distracted him. There were two armed guards on the plane—members of the Royal New Zealand Air Force, Scott assumed. They had little hats and carried handguns in shoulder holsters over baby-blue shirts. One of them—the one who'd just stood—had a pink breast cancer awareness pin on his lapel, and Scott's heart leaped up into his throat.

"Um," Scott said, and he considered for a moment whether to say anything. Sometimes a breast cancer pin is just a breast cancer pin. Sometimes a crazy look in someone's eye is just a crazy look in someone's eye. *Yep,* Scott thought, *I should have said something.*

The airman drew his weapon now, and aimed it at his counterpart.

"Unholster it slow and slide it up the aisle at me, Nigel!" shouted the airman. "I'm serious," he added, and there was no doubt about that. He had the glassy, up-all-night look of someone with no sense of humor at all.

Nigel did as he was told, and the other airman stopped the second pistol under his shoe.

"Let's talk, mate," said Nigel. "Nobody's done anythi—"

"Shut up! Shut up! All of you—" he said, waving his gun at the people near the front of the cabin behind him, the people who had been helping Queen Elizabeth with her video hookup. "Get to the rear of the plane! I want everybody together!"

"He's a Freeman," John whispered. "Look at his pin."

Everyone was in the back now. Everyone, Scott noted, except the queen. He'd lost track of her.

"I don't care what you are," said Nigel to his fellow airman. "First and foremost you are an officer of the Royal Air Force, and your loyalty is to—"

The airman raised his pistol even with Nigel's head, his arm trembling.

"My loyalty . . . my loyalty is to the Lady of the Lake."

"His mind isn't his own," said Mick. "Bet yeh all the Freemen eat plenty o' Goodco cereal. Sure an' he's one o' Nimue's sugar zombies, now."

"Where our Lady leads . . . we must follow."

That made Scott remember the Tower of London, and the ravens—poor creatures, bound by a common spell, forced to follow and find Titania's court whenever it vanished.

He'd noticed that his mind had a stupid tendency to wander during mortal danger—it was why he'd never be a decent action hero.

"I'm sorry, Nigel," said the airman. "You've never acted against my lady." Then he frowned. "But you never joined the Freemen when I asked you to either, so maybe you deserve this. I don't know, whatever. I'm crashing all of us into the ocean."

"Any ideas?" said Scott.

"I have plenty o' glamour these days," whispered Mick. "That'll protect us."

"Protect *us*," said Merle, "or just protect you? Maybe your glamour'll make the bullet bounce off your big metal zipper and hit me in the head."

Mick winced and shrugged.

"*You* could maybe do something," Scott said to Haskoll. "If you decided to. You could take his gun away from him."

"Not unless it's magical. I tried to explain that on the ice—I only seem to be able to touch magical things. I couldn't keep my grip on your hand 'cause you're barely a changeling."

"Talkin' to your imaginary friend?" asked Mick.

"*You're* my imaginary friend. I have imaginary enemies now."

Merle jumped in his seat, like he'd been goosed. He coughed nervously.

The airman with the gun was crying. "Here's what's going to happen," he said. "I'm going to shoot my way into the cockpit and kill the pilots and point us at the sea. I . . . I'll try to make it quick."

Scott noticed a red slip of something appear by his foot. The red merrow's cap John had told him about—the thing that could make a person torpedo through the water, just by thinking about it. John had slid it backward, under his seat. Scott clamped it between his sneakers and lifted it as inconspicuously as possible into his hand.

What was the plan here? Was he supposed to give it to Mick? Was its magic useful somehow? Then, with a start, Scott realized it was only a life preserver. If Scott survived the crash, he might be able to use this cap to whisk him to land. His heart went soft in him. His father didn't own *two* caps.

What they really needed was the magic of the tower, Scott thought. He needed to be able to whisk himself away and have everyone he loved follow safely behind. He needed Polly in the same universe and his mother back from the void, by his side. He needed his dad—a living dad, a dad who wasn't always trying to sacrifice himself for Scott's sake, or for Polly's. He needed Merle and the pixies and he needed King Arthur and his magical sword to finally appear like he was *supposed* to and save the day.

Oh, thought Scott as the Arthur question drifted through his mind. *Oh. So maybe* that's *the problem.*

"Oh, airman," said a voice, the queen's voice. Scott still couldn't see where she was.

The airman couldn't either. He waved his gun, squinting at all the faces.

"There's a tradition when you meet the queen, or king," said Elizabeth. Her voice wasn't so far away from Scott, but it was on the move. "Like so many of the old traditions," she continued, "it isn't observed as often as it once was, but it is said that one mustn't show their back in the presence of royalty. I expect you've forgotten this, airman, if ever you knew it."

"Your . . . Majesty—" said the airman.

"Hush. I'm not finished. It can be quite amusing,

everyone walking backward out of rooms all the time—but there is a point to it. Most possibly assume the point is one of old-fashioned respect, but I rather think it's about personal safety."

Elizabeth appeared in the aisle now from between two seats, several feet behind the man with the gun.

"You keep an eye on her, because the queen must be watched. The queen is *dangerous*."

The airman pivoted, turned to step toward her, but his shoelaces were tied together. He dropped like a felled tree at her feet.

"Don't turn your back on the queen, airman," she said, before waving Merle's wand in his face.

COMMERCIAL BREAK

KID
That crazy rabbit
is at it again!

KID
He thinks Madam Fortuna
can tell him the secret
ingredient that gives
Honey Frosted Snox! its
delicious magic!

SNOX RABBIT
Do you thee anything
in your crythtal ball?!

MADAM FORTUNA
The delicious Snox
magic was taken from
beasts of the earth
and air! Unicorns!
Griffins! *DRAGONS!*

KID
Stupid rabbit! Kids
know that the delicious
taste comes from magic
honeycombs—

SNOX RABBIT
No. No, she's right.
Thacrifithes were made.

SNOX RABBIT
They took magic from me
too, you know. Thtored
it away, where it pickled
like eggth in a thellar.

KID
Um—

SNOX RABBIT
They thtored the magic
until our Lady could
gorge herthelf on it,
uthe it to tear a hole
in the belly of the
world.

KID
This isn't how these...
how these commercials
usually—

SNOX RABBIT
Can you feel it thtarting?
You're going to walk
through that tear tho that
one of my friendth can
come here.

KID
That's not fair.

SNOX RABBIT
It *is*. We're allowed
to thteal children,
replace them with a
changeling. We've
alwayth thtolen
children.

SNOX RABBIT
Can't change dethtiny.
Go now. Oblivion awaitth.

VOICEOVER
Another good cereal
from the good folks
at Goodco!
There's a Little Bit
of Magic in Every Box!

CHAPTER 23

Everything was pink.

Behind her eyes, inside her eyes; filling the cracks of her mind, pooling in the fissures.

Emily sailed through the air in the arms of a monster and couldn't remember what she'd been thinking about. Harvey, maybe? Her mind had gone to commercial.

The monster also carried a man she'd once thought of as her father and a boy she'd once considered her brother. It was a very capable monster. It landed feet-first on the roof of a car, crumpling the frame, and rolled onto the hood. The tight knot of bodies came apart, and Erno and Mr. Wilson tumbled to the pavement. They were a bit battered, but they picked themselves up all the same.

Emily was not battered. The pink had coursed out of her, surrounded her, protected her.

The monster (*Biggs. His name is Biggs.*) rose and stared

at her. He looked weary—weary in his body, weary in his soul. Erno and Mr. Wilson stared at her too, with something like interest.

"You're flying," Erno told her.

Oh. So she was.

It didn't feel like flying. It felt like she was being held aloft, but she couldn't see the wires.

"Your eyes are pink," Erno added.

"They were always pink," she said.

"Not the pupils."

"Still shooting at us," said Biggs, and that was true. They had the cover of the car, and of the other cars around them in this parking lot, but bullets were chipping the asphalt, shattering windows, cracking taillights all around them. It didn't seem like such a big deal suddenly.

"Something's happened," Erno said, and he screwed up his face, trying to get a grip on this something.

"The spell's been cast," said Mr. Wilson. "The Lady of the Lake is drafting her army, and it's us."

Emily drifted over their heads, toward the bridge that spanned the lake and stretched into town.

"Emily, hold up!" said Erno, and he loped after her. Biggs and Mr. Wilson followed, and Erno looked over his shoulder at them. "What do you mean, it's us? I'm not joining Nimue's army."

"Are you having trouble thinking?" asked Mr. Wilson. "Are you having trouble even caring? We've all been feeding ourselves Milk-Seven, or just Goodco cereals, for years. You used to eat Puftees every morning."

Biggs could have caught Emily easily; instead he shuffled his feet as though snarled by misery.

Erno rattled his head, tried to clear his mind. Emily had already made it to the entrance of the bridge. Beyond the water lay Goodborough. The lights of the fogbound town looked like a kind of fairy kingdom to him now. They cast a dull pumpkin glow on the underside of a low cloud and pierced the belly of it here and there with spires like spear points.

"Forget it, Erno," said Mr. Wilson. "Forget it." He sagged, and tried to hoist a heavy hand onto Erno's shoulder. "Let her go. It's over."

"OH MY GOD SHUT UP!" Erno answered. "This is all your fault, you don't get to decide when it's over. There! Golf cart!"

There was a fleet of white golf carts at the edge of the lot. Erno tumbled into the first of these, pressed the starter, and with an electric whir, he scooted toward the bridge. After a moment he glanced in the mirror and was relieved to see that Biggs and Mr. Wilson had climbed into the next two carts and were close behind.

Up ahead, in the night air, Emily shone like a pink

lantern through the fog. She'd be swallowed up, save for a faint shimmer in the mist, and Erno would almost lose her. But the fog would roil and there she'd be again, a barefoot girl in the sky, reflected in the slick surface of the bridge below.

"Emily!"

She was nearly across now, and a bridge cable snapped. The bundled metal of it just gave up, lashed backward from its mooring and cut spirals through the fog. Then another cable snapped, and the masonry of the bridge itself began to crumble.

It was the noise of it all that reached Erno first—the Star Wars sounds of the metal cables trilling with all that pent-up tension, the fog-muffled grind of a thousand tons of stone cracking loose and falling into the lake. He turned his head and saw Mr. Wilson drop off the edge, golf cart and all. Just like that—no scream, no famous last words. The bridge just dropped out from under him, and he was gone.

"Emily," Erno whispered. "What did you do?"

Biggs was all right—he and Erno managed to urge their carts just ahead of the destruction and entered Goodborough as the last of the bridge decayed and tumbled into the water.

The road curved, sharply, and Erno turned into a skid, lost control, tipped the cart. Biggs screeched to a halt

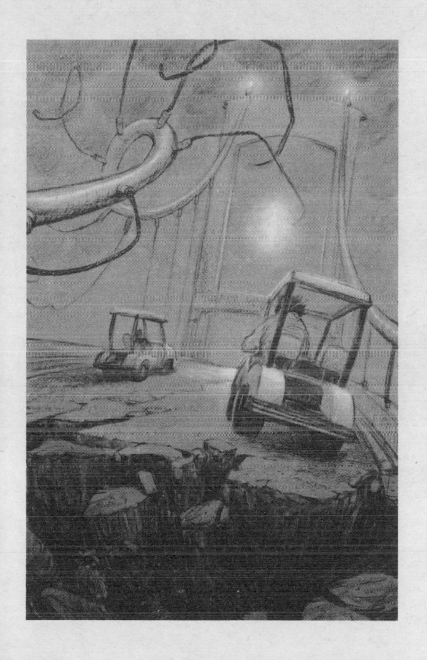

beside him and got out.

"Mr. Wilson," said the shaggy giant.

"I know," Erno said, breathing hard as he crawled free of the golf cart. Biggs picked it up and put it right again.

"Sorry."

"It's . . . ," Erno began. But it wasn't okay. He didn't know what it was. Mr. Wilson, gone again. Gone for good.

"The file said he was my dad," Erno told Biggs. "My real dad. The file said my mom died when I was born and he . . . gave up. Gave me up, I mean."

"Nimue lies," said Biggs, and the big man put a loose hand on Erno's shoulder.

"Yeah," said Erno. He pressed his palms into his eyes— he wanted to sleep. "Yeah. Where's Emily?" he added. Now they were surrounded by the stores and buildings of the lakefront, and he couldn't see her anymore. "Wait, is that . . ."

There was a girl walking in the middle of the road, a block away. She was in a nightgown, but she wasn't glowing. Or floating.

"Someone else," said Biggs. "Emily's gone."

"She's not gone. Come on, that's the cereal talking."

Biggs looked like he was about to just sit down in the road.

"No, please, get up. Get in the cart—I'll drive it," Erno

said. He pulled at Biggs's hairy arm.

He got the man up, finally, and he wheeled the cart down the block with Biggs hanging out the back. The girl in the nightgown was barefoot and shivering, her face a blank.

"Hey," Erno said to her over the whir of the motor. "Hey, um. I'm Erno."

But she didn't give any indication that she could tell he was there. She began to make a shuffling left turn, and when Erno peered down that block he saw the figures of more children, maybe a teenager in his boxers and a T-shirt, all doddering in the same direction. And the pale pink light of his sister, vanishing into the fog.

There was a tremble in the earth. Erno had never felt a tremor before, and the city boy in him took it for the rattle of a passing truck. But it was almost four in the morning, and the streets were deserted but for sleepwalkers.

"We can catch her," Erno said.

He jerked the wheel right and left, threading a path between the children—a boy in airplane pajamas, twins walking hand-in-hand with running noses, a girl with a stuffed rabbit in her hands, absently tearing it to pieces. Its foot dropped as Erno passed, but he left it in the street—didn't seem like good luck, tonight.

And now the fog swirled, and Emily was visible again, pink, pale against an indigo sky that sagged with lumps of dark cloud. Clouds like Erno had never seen—black marshmallows, sinking like dying balloons. The ground shook again, and lightning flashed pink—*pink lightning*—and for a moment Erno saw something colossal in the distance. The rift. He shouldn't have been able to see it, but there it was, all the sky bent around it.

The rising wind stung his eyes as he narrowed the gap between the cart and the pink specter of his sister hovering ahead.

"Biggs?"

The big man didn't need much urging this time. With Emily in sight he climbed atop the speeding golf cart and braced himself against the rush of air that whipped his fur all around him. The light of her neared, and grew stronger, much stronger, and Emily turned her head.

"Uh . . . ," said Erno.

Then Biggs leaped off the top of the golf cart, and wrapped Emily in his arms.

CHAPTER 24

The plane set down in Los Angeles and didn't bother taxiing up to the terminal. Instead it came to a halt on another runway, far out from any buildings or passenger planes, but alongside three sleek black jets that looked like Batman's private fleet.

"Blackbirds." John whistled as he squinted out the window at them. "They're not messing around. These'll get us to New Jersey in . . . I don't know, an *hour*."

"Why three?" asked Mick.

"Well, I think they normally only carry two people. The pilot and somebody else."

They all disembarked down a staircase to the tarmac. Scott glanced at the queen, who appeared to be speaking to someone's tablet computer. He caught a glimpse of the President of the United States on the screen, looking grave.

Elizabeth broke off and addressed them.

"It's dire," she said. "Millions of children missing or marching in the streets. Millions more being confined like mad dogs by their frightened families. And adults too—in the streets, or behaving strangely."

"Adults who eat children's cereal?" said John.

"Probably," Merle said. "But Goodco makes more than cereal. They make Velveteen Cheese Loaf. Belasco Hot Sauce. You know Kobold Snacks? With the commercials where all the gnomes live underground in a cookie mine? That's Goodco too."

"There are already some ten thousand children gathered at a particular spot in Goodborough, New Jersey," the queen continued. "And a small army of armed Freemen there as well."

"Guarding the new rift, certainly."

"No doubt. But law enforcement is reluctant, for the children's sake, to move in and spark a firefight. Meanwhile, New Jersey is having some strange weather, and more than the customary number of earthquakes. And those phenomena seem to be spreading."

Merle frowned. "That doesn't sound right. Why would that be?"

"'S like the spell isn't stable," said Mick. "Like maybe we weakened Nimue just enough that she can't keep it under control."

John looked back and forth. "So what does that mean?"

There was a moment of silence.

Merle said, "When I was a kid, my mom and dad told me all about the day the elves appeared. They never mentioned the weather or earthquakes. This is different."

"Well, that's good!" John announced. "Right? That means we made a difference after all! Your future isn't just going to play out all over again."

"Could be good," Mick allowed. "Whole thing could come apart like a wet napkin. Or it could come apart like an A-bomb."

They fell into an uneasy silence again.

Scott, for his part, had been silent all along—he had his nose in maps. He looked at all the known rifts on Earth, compared those to the ones he knew in Pretannica, traced paths with his finger, circled spots with a pen.

"What're you doing there?" Merle asked finally.

"The lad thinks he's figured somethin' out," Mick told Merle. "So far that's all I've been able t' get out o' him."

"Shhh!" Scott hissed, waving his hand. "Can't concentrate!"

"So let us help," said Merle. "What's this about?"

"I . . . think I've thought of a way to bring the worlds back together."

Merle shook his head and pulled something from the

pocket of his robe. "*This* is how we're merging the worlds again," he said.

"What is that?" Mick said, wincing at it. "Ham radio?"

Merle clucked his tongue. "It's—it's not as elegant as I'd like, I admit that, but I didn't have much time, or the best tools to work with—"

"It's a new time device," said Scott.

It was another octagonal ring, about twice the size of the one that had taken Scott's mom into the future. It had one of Mick's gold coins at each corner, and a mess of circuits and capacitors sticking every which way.

"Not quite," said Merle. "It's not precise enough for that. But look . . . if it was my device that split the worlds, then it'll be my device that brings them back together again. This little toaster will establish a tachyon sync with the chronological event horizon of the Gloria—"

"Okay," said Scott, "whatever. I hope it works. But if it doesn't—"

"It will."

"If it doesn't," said Scott, "then I have a plan too. I need that hat," he added, turning about. "Where's that red hat?"

"The merrow's cap?" asked Mick. "'S in your pocket."

Scott reached back and felt the silky ear of the cap hanging out of the hip pocket of his jeans. "I'm about to try something really crazy and dumb," he said.

"Sounds abou' right," said the leprechaun. "Want some company?"

"I wish I could say yes. But I don't think it's gonna work with two people. Your Majesty?"

"Young man," answered the queen.

"I need to get to the Grand Canyon as quickly as possible. Do you think you could call in another favor?"

CHAPTER 25

Biggs plucked Emily out of the air like an apple from a tree, and the two of them tumbled to the street as Erno swerved to avoid them. Then Biggs was a cloud of butterflies, and Emily stepped lightly out of this cloud and turned. Then the butterflies were Biggs again. Then the pink lightning came down and struck the big man, struck the golf cart, pockmarked the street.

Erno held his breath, but he was unharmed—the cart's rubber wheels insulated him against the lightning. He thought, grimly, that if there was anything left of his sister in that glowing shell, she would have known that.

Biggs smelled like burned hair. He staggered to his big feet, all his fur sticking off at right angles, then dropped again. He lay in the road as silent children scuffled by him, and didn't get up.

Emily turned her attention to Erno. Erno sat in his golf cart.

"Emily . . . ," he said. "I . . . I know you won't hurt me."

A little boy passed, trailing cereal puffs. Erno stepped out of the cart. A woman somewhere called the name Ashley again and again, with rising panic. Emily watched Erno, motionless but for her hair (which was in a frenzy), the tips of her toes not quite touching the ground.

"Look," Erno went on, "Biggs needs help." The big man's chest was (he thought) still rising and falling. "You can . . . help me help him. Let's get him into this golf cart."

The earth rumbled again. The windows of apartment buildings all around them splintered. Car alarms wailed distantly but from every direction.

Erno stepped closer. "No? You don't want to help Biggs? Biggs, who carried you when you got dizzy? And got you your first library card? Look. It's still him, he just needs a haircut. We all need haircuts. And new clothes, and a house where we can start over."

He was close enough to touch her now. He *did* touch her, with a trembling hand, then hugged her—quickly, like his resolve might fail him. Like ripping off a Band-Aid. He squeezed her tight, and still she just stood there—until the pink coursed out of her again, and came between them, and swatted Erno away. It tossed him like he was weightless, like he was nothing, and he caromed off the golf cart with a sharp crack. When he landed, he landed heavily. Dead weight.

In every cartoon she'd missed out on when she was younger, in every comic book and movie, this was the moment when the mind control would be broken. Having been forced to hurt someone she loved, Emily would blink, shake her head. Then, with the full realization of what she'd done, she would run to Erno's side, shake her fist at the villain. "It's over, Nimue," she'd say. "I'll never be your puppet again."

That didn't happen here. Instead, Emily daydreamed.

She pictured a plain gray room, empty save for a chair in the middle. A plain gray chair in an empty room—she'd dreamed of this before.

After a moment, a girl who looked just like Emily entered and took her seat.

"You again," Emily said to the girl.

"You remember," said the girl. "That's good. I was afraid you were too far gone to remember. But then, if you were too far gone, I guess you wouldn't have found your way in here."

"You don't have your headgear anymore."

"I never did."

"The last time I saw you, you told me something terrible was going to happen."

The girl nodded. "And look at you—you're something terrible, all right."

Silence. A slight warbling hum, as if everything beyond this room were just wind and nothing.

"That was you in my head in Wilson's row house in London too, wasn't it? The last time Nimue stepped in. You got me to touch the four-leaf clover and break her spell, you clever thing. You meddlesome little—"

"Stop that. You're talking like *her*. We don't talk like that."

Emily studied the girl for a moment. She really was a remarkable imitation. In fact, Emily noted, with no small amount of bile, that the girl in the chair was a flawed copy only in the sense that she seemed perfectly, placidly calm. No one who knew Emily would ever mistake her for calm.

"Who *are* you?"

"You don't know?" the girl said, tilting her head. "I'm the real you. I'm the little sliver of your brain that the Milk never touched. I'm the girl you would have been if you'd never taken the Milk at all—happy, whole."

"I'm smarter than you."

"In some ways."

"So ignorance is bliss, is that what you're telling me? That I'd be happier being sweet and dumb? That's disgusting."

"There's more than one kind of intelligence, Emily," said the girl. "The Milk made you smart, but it could never make you wise. Knowledge without wisdom can only make you miserable. Not that I'm so happy at the moment, of course—you're killing my brother—"

"He was never our brother."

"See, now, that's a perfect example. With all your smarts, you only recently figured that out. I've *always* known that he wasn't our brother—just as I've always known that, in every way that mattered, he was."

The wind howled, now. The wind sobbed.

"Is. Not was, is."

"There you go."

"That noise . . . that's not the wind, is it?"

The girl—the other Emily was close now. Her face was close, though she hadn't moved from her chair.

"No," she said. "That's not the wind. That's you. That's us."

Closer. Closer still.

"I . . . I can't tell which one of us I am."

"Good. That's good. Go tell that to the world."

She woke, sobbing, and saw a street filled with kids. Kids, and a few adults—adults half dressed and holding their bodies tight as they tried to make sense of what they were seeing. Some of these kids walked right past her without a glance. One kid in particular lay motionless by a golf cart.

"Oh no," Emily whispered.

She tried to move, but the pink wouldn't let her. It filled her veins, tried to harden her heart.

"No," Emily growled. "You're through. You've had your fun. Now *me*."

It started with a finger, then her hand. Then a deep breath, and she shook herself loose. She lost her balance, but it was *her* balance now. She fell on her hands, got up again, rushed to Erno's side.

His heart felt weak. Her heart felt weak, too.

"Hey!" said a man down the street. He moved toward her in sweatpants and slippers. "Kid! Girl! What's going on, why are all these kids out here?" He crouched by her now. "There's a . . . bigfoot or something over there," he added. "Is that boy hurt? Do you want me to call 911?"

Emily leaned over Erno and put her hands on his chest.

"Kid . . . ," said the man. "You know you're glowing a little? What . . . what *is* that?"

Magic, she thought. *Isn't that ridiculous? Magic.* She tried to shape it. She tried to tell it what to do.

Just like in a movie. Just like in a cartoon.

CHAPTER 26

They couldn't land in Philadelphia—it was too close to the maelstrom, and the pilots spotted at least two types of clouds that no one had ever heard of before, so they ended up setting down at McGuire Air Force Base, to the northeast of Goodborough. John and Merle and Mick and the queen were helped down to the tarmac, whereupon John apologized about his helmet.

"I was, ah . . . sick in that," he told an airman. "A few times. You should just get rid of it."

To say that Mick kissed the ground didn't even begin to describe his affections.

"You think air force pilots always feel like that?" asked Merle, staggering. A member of the ground crew had to hold him up. "It's like you an' physics are having a disagreement, and you're losing."

Mick rolled over onto his back and composed a spontaneous ode:

> *"O blessed ground, so sound an' sturdy,*
> *Spare the air for bat an' birdie—*
> *Let them keep those lofty things*
> *That want not feet, but beating wings.*
> *An' to my grave, I'll gravely swear*
> *By terra firma, firm an' fair."*

"If you are quite finished," said the queen, unruffled.

Mick wasn't finished, and he continued to praise the ground in rhyme and song until he saw that they were being led to a helicopter.

Emily raced through the streets of Goodborough, pausing intermittently to give exasperated looks over her shoulder.

"Can't you guys go any faster?" she said. "The world's gonna end without us!"

Biggs loped along, his fur frazzled, the ends split and burned. Erno was still limping, but she swore he was favoring a different leg.

"Give us a break," he groaned. "We were dead recently."

"Oh, you were never dead."

"Pretty sure I was," said Erno. "Killed by my own sister. Killed with magic."

"And then healed with the same magic, so no harm, no foul."

A unicorn galloped past, wild of eye. It's typically hard to read a unicorn's expression, but this one was as transparently confused as you'd expect a unicorn to be upon finding itself in a blue-collar town in southwestern New Jersey.

Emily traced its path backward and pointed. "Look! There it is!"

"It" turned out to be a crowd of people, mostly parents who were screaming and crying and carrying on. And no wonder—they were being held at bay by pink men with guns, and those men were circling an ever-growing multitude of the parents' children. The mob of them must have filled ten city blocks.

The sky churned overhead, revealing a void that was black and dead in its center.

"I don't think there's . . . anything we can do here," said Erno, panting.

"I wonder. Maybe I can do something with my, you know, magic."

"How much do you suppose you have left?"

"I don't know."

"I wonder how you'd even measure something like that."

"Based on how all my doctor's appointments at Goodco

used to go," Emily said, "I'm gonna guess 'pee in a cup.'"

The ring of parents was like a single, teeming creature, an undulating coral reef of misery. A nearby father was pleading, "Jacob! Jacob, please come back. Come back to Daddy. I'm sorry I yelled, Jacob!" Then he flinched and moved quickly aside as a tall elf, wearing a dress of rose petals, stepped lithely from the pulsating crowd. She paused to admire Emily as if she were a rare flower.

It made Emily feel creepy, so she moved Erno and Biggs some distance away.

"I feel like Mr. Wilson would know what to do," Emily said. "I mean, he's gone weird in the head, but he obviously knew more about Goodco than anybody. I wish we knew what he was planning."

"Yeah," said Erno. He moved restlessly on the balls of his feet. "All he said was, 'I have an idea!' Then he turned his golf cart around and drove back onto Goodco's island while you were still all pink and floaty."

Emily looked vague. "Did I . . . did I collapse the bridge?" she asked.

"Uh . . . yeah."

"It's so hard to remember. That means Mr. Wilson is stuck on the island. I trapped him there."

Erno looked as though he might answer, but they were all distracted by the passage of a dark helicopter overhead, charting a woozy curve through all this fickle

weather. Erno squinted.

"That was an Iroquois," he said. "U.S. military. Look, there's a couple more farther off."

"Then that's where we're going," said Emily with sudden resolve. "We're going to find where they land and offer our help. Biggs? Are you feeling up to carrying me? My legs are tired and I can't remember how to fly."

In the helicopter, they huddled as they buzzed a path over the treetops toward Goodborough.

"I wish I understood what Scott was up to," John shouted over the wind. "Why the Grand Canyon?"

"I've been wondering that, too," said Merle.

"I have an inklin'," said Mick. "Trust the boy. He'll save all us miserable so-an'-sos, given half a chance."

"Gentlemen," said the queen. "I think I see our rift."

They peered out the open door and through the gaps between buildings and saw a throng of people down below, thousands of bodies clustered around a central point. Children, mostly. Men in pink rubber suits too. And desperate parents, surging at the edges. The bodies had formed an aisle—an empty spoke leading from the center to the fringe—and as they watched, a fresh body walked down that aisle. Something neither child nor Freeman.

"Did you see that?" said John.

"That was an elf," said Mick, squinting. "Just appeared where one o' the kids'd been standing a second ago. An' look there—a giant. I think I know that guy."

"A dragon or something," said John, pointing. "Just a little one. There."

The helicopter veered away from this scene, toward the spot in the park that Merle had marked on a map. When it set down on the lawn it was followed by another helicopter, and then another. Soldiers or airmen streamed out of these and formed a perimeter. But it appeared they had nothing to defend against—the Freemen either didn't know about this spot, or didn't care.

Merle ambled around, looking down, then up at the line of buildings south of the park, then down again. "Here," he said.

"You're sure?" said John.

"Sure as I can be. This is just about where I first appeared, fresh from the Middle Ages. This is where King Arthur should have appeared too." Merle readied his new device—the tiny jalopy of a time machine that he'd thrown together from parts at McMurdo Station.

"So what's the plan here?" asked Mick.

"It was my device that fractured everything apart. It'll be my device that'll put all the pieces together again. This is gonna act like a receiver—it'll close the loop, and both Earth and Pretannica will merge into the single world they were always meant to be."

"And then we shall have an elf problem," said the queen. "Forgive me for saying so, Mick—but Merle, you come from a time that also had a sudden and unexpected influx of the Fay, and it led to hegemony."

"It led to what now?" asked Mick.

"To the Fay taking over everything," said Merle. "What can we do? They won't have their big pink dragon this time. Maybe that'll make a difference."

"And maybe it won't, sir," said a man in fatigues—one of the soldiers, armed and serious. "Your weird little group has been given free rein until now, but now we wait. The United Nations Security Council is in an emergency meeting, and I have my orders not to let you act until they've made their decision."

More men stood nearby, menacing without trying to look menacing.

"Look, soldier—" said John.

"Marine, sir."

"Sorry. Marine. Look at the sky. Feel the air here. This is all going very wrong, and we don't have a lot of time—"

"That isn't your call to make. Sir."

"So whose call is it? All those people who've been saying I'm crazy these past six months?" said John, stepping forward.

"My wife likes your albums, sir. Please don't make me shoot you."

"Is that what you'd do," said Merle, "if I tried to turn this thing on? Shoot me?"

The marine didn't answer right away. He grimaced into the howling wind.

"Those are my orders," he said.

"You'd better get to it, then," said Merle. "I flipped the switch two minutes ago."

The marine raised his rifle.

"You can't kill me, you know," said Merle. "I haven't even been born yet."

"Drop the device!"

Merle shrugged and tossed it at his feet. "It didn't work," he said. "I thought it would work, but it didn't."

The big man lowered his weapon, just as the earth growled and rumbled, as if hungry. As if it could swallow them all up. They toppled onto the grass. The marine looked up at the sky as if for the first time.

"So . . . so what do we do now?" he asked them. They all found their footing again.

"Now . . . we try Plan B," John said.

"Stormin' the castle," said Mick.

CHAPTER 27

Emily and Erno and Biggs arrived at the edge of the park just in time to watch two of the three helicopters leave.

There was a dark gash across the sky. Pink lightning flashed through it, and it flashed inside Emily's mind as well. For an instant she was back in the fishbowl room, and the fishbowl was shattered. The decoy doll that Mr. Wilson had placed inside was burning, and the whole room, the whole vast room, was charged, firing off impulses like a titanic brain. In the center of the room, a woman was on fire and screaming.

Emily blinked, and she was back in the park again with another gun in her face.

"My *God*, am I tired of guns," she said.

The marines who had been left here must have been new recruits. Like many kids, Emily often mistook anyone over sixteen for an adult—but these men were frightened, and when they were frightened they looked like boys playing dress-up.

"What is that?" said one, meaning Biggs. "What is that?"

"Big hairy man," whispered another.

Emily scowled at them. "This is Brian Macintyre Biggs. He is my nanny and a librarian and his taxes pay your wages, so you will show him *respect*."

Biggs, who had his massive hands in the air, jiggled one of them.

The marines' postures seemed to relax, slightly. They were used to being spoken to like this. Not by little girls specifically, but still.

"Miss," said the lead man. "It's not safe to be out tonight. Please, all of you, return to your homes. We are in this park because of a . . ."

"Training exercise," suggested another marine.

"We are here for a training exercise. There is nothing to worry ab—"

"You're here because you're guarding that," Emily said with a gesture to the intricate ring on the ground. "It's an improvised time-traveling device made by one Merle Lynn that he thought would integrate Earth with a magical world of fairies and elves. But it didn't."

The marine screwed up his face, groaned at his men. "Oh, come *on*! Does *everyone* know more about what's going on than us?"

"This is nothing," said Erno. "Ask her to guess what number you're thinking of."

"So they left you to guard the device," Emily added, "just in case it suddenly works, which it won't. And the others left to confront Nimue inside Goodco headquarters in the middle of Lake Meer."

Just then the ground shook again, and not just the ground—the trees, the air; the secret strings that tie everything together. You may wonder how a person would notice that last one, but when it happens you just know.

The lightning had ignited the sky, and now the sky was on fire.

"It's too late." Emily shuddered. "They're going to be too late."

In their Iroquois helicopter they balanced in the air above Lake Meer. The other chopper had drifted ahead and engaged the enemy—the enemy being a mere dozen Freemen firing rifles from the roof. These Freemen were subdued quickly and laid down their weapons.

"This is great," said Merle. "Why didn't we do it this way all along? With a private army, I mean."

"Because everyone else on Earth thought we were mad," said John.

Freemen were streaming out of the headquarters to

the edge of the bridge, which of course was ruined. Some of them were taking their chances in the water, attempting to swim across.

"Even they can tell somethin's wrong," said Mick. "The rats're desertin' the ship."

John pointed at the bridge, or rather the lack of it. "Did you lot do that?" he asked the staff sergeant.

"Negative. I was about to ask you the same question."

They landed on the roof and established a perimeter, and Merle asked, "What does that mean, actually? Establishing a perimeter," and the staff sergeant got somebody less important to explain it to him, and then John and Merle and Mick were rushed down a stairwell and into Goodco headquarters.

"I'm getting word," said the staff sergeant with his hand up to his ear, "that the Freemen in the city are losing control of the children. It's like the kids are waking up."

"Nimue's losin' control of everythin'," said Mick.

"Yes, sir. Also the sky is on fire."

They all shared a look.

Up ahead and around the corner, men were shouting. John and Merle and Mick were waved ahead, and they saw a Freeman with his hands in the air.

"It's all falling apart!" he was shouting. "You have to stop her! It isn't happening like we were told!"

Merle stepped forward. "Okay, calm down. We're

gonna fix this, but you have to tell us where she is."

"Yeah. Yeah. She's in a room in the center of the fifth—"

A shot was fired, a head-splitting noise in these close quarters, and the Freemen crumpled. This was immediately followed by the marines raising their weapons in unison, a gruff chorus of men shouting "Drop it! Drop it!" Eventually they disarmed another, more familiar Freeman in a black cowboy hat.

"I recognize this one," said Mick to Merle.

"Right," Merle agreed. "From the Philly airport."

John was outraged. "You shot that man in the back!"

"That man was a traitor," the Freeman with the black hat said as marines bound his wrists and ankles with plastic ties. "A traitor to all humanity."

"You prat," said John. "We would have found her eventually anyway, with or without his help."

"You got that right," said Mick. "I can feel it below us. It's buzzin' up through the floor."

The staff sergeant scowled at the Freeman. "Leave him," he said. "Let the next wave clean up the garbage."

Erno jerked backward as another marine approached their group carrying a tiny Queen Elizabeth like a ventriloquist's dummy. Then Emily and Biggs bowed, so Erno shrugged and bowed too.

"Your Majesty," said Emily.

"You must be Emily," said the queen. "You appear unsurprised by my size."

"I assumed you'd look something like this."

Erno sighed and rolled his eyes. This gave him an unplanned glimpse of the fierce and fiery sky, which he'd been trying to avoid looking at, so he focused on the tiny queen again.

"I'm told you're in possession of a rare and gifted brain," the tiny queen continued. "Have you any thoughts about our predicament?"

Emily tightened up a little. "My brain isn't what it used to be," she said, and looked down at Merle's octagonal ring on the ground. "It wasn't a bad instinct, trying to close the loop like this. I'm embarrassed to say that I'm currently full of magic—I could try to give it a boost, but I still think something's missing. Some piece of the puz—"

Emily froze, then placed a finger against the wire of her headgear.

"What?" said Erno with a grin. "What is it? I know that look—you've figured out what we need to do!"

"Yes," said Emily. "I've figured out what we need to do." She grimaced and hugged her feeble body. "I've figured it out, and it's *impossible*."

On the fifth floor they could all feel it; it was like walking into an oven. Waves of glamour radiated out from the hot center. And as they trod through the high-arched corridors, they came across more Freemen—Freemen lying facedown, Freemen folded into uncomfortable shapes, Freemen with some aspect of them changed by wild magic. One was wearing a dress, another was growing mushrooms from his face, still another was just an orangutan in a robe. One had been made so monstrously large that he would have been terrifying if he wasn't already dead. Still, they had to thread their way past him single file.

The magic affected Mick first. He doubled over as if he'd been hurt, but he came up laughing. His gnarled old face was nearly split by an agonizing grin, and he began to dance around and clap his hands.

"O lads, I cannot take much more.
I've only so much time before
I caper till I'm out o' breath
An' laugh myself to death.

"This glamour's filled me like a cup.
I'll jig until the jig is up,
An' cackle till my face goes purple,
Nothing rhymes with purple.

"I'll—"

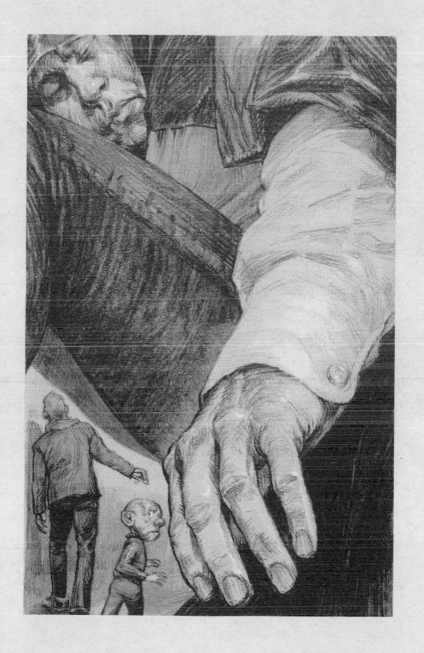

But here Merle grabbed his shoulders and shook him. "Snap out of it!" he said. "We're gonna need you in there!"

"Maybe he should just get to safety," said John.

"No . . . ," said Mick, panting. "No, I'm all right, lads. Heeee! Sorry. I can . . . heh . . . I can hold it together."

They all kept an eye on Mick as they advanced. "What's the situation?" the staff sergeant asked John under his breath.

"He's a leprechaun," John answered. "We probably should have explained that before. He's a magical being, and all this wild magic is making him a bit . . ."

"Drunk? Annoying?"

"HA!" barked Mick.

"I was going to say 'spirited.' Anyway, I'm worried it's going to get to me next."

The big marine raised an eyebrow. "Why would that be?"

"I'm part fairy," said John. There was a quiet pause, and he eyed the man. "Is that a problem?"

"No, sir. The United States military is very accepting of that sort of thing nowadays."

Holes started to appear in the walls they passed. Then wide swaths of the walls and ceiling were absent—not fragmented or collapsed, just gone. The corridor lights flickered, and here and there water or air spilled out of riddled ductwork.

"What's that noise?" asked John. "That high-pitched sound—it keeps getting louder."

Soon they turned a corner that was barely a corner, passed a Freeman made of tubers lying next to a half wall, and then they could see her. The Lady of the Lake, the Godmother.

"Oh," said John, "it was her. That sound was her."

She was screaming in the center of the vast ruins of several rooms, white flares and pink fire swirling around her. Wreckage, unrecognizable debris everywhere. The fairy queen herself was like a bright ghost, a diaphanous spirit of light. What was left of the magical machine, with its golden batteries, oscillated around her. The staff sergeant squinted at it.

"What is that?" he muttered.

"Sort of a magical backup generator," said Merle. "Based on my own designs, I'm sorry to say. Shoot those golden parts out of it, and we might be able to end this thing quick."

"Heeheeeee!" said Mick.

"Heh," said John, and then he stifled an explosive laugh behind his hand. "Sorry. Good plan. My laughter has no bearing on the plan."

"Jefferson!" called the staff sergant, and a marksman with a long, lean rifle stepped forward. "You heard the man."

"Yes, sir."

Jefferson took a knee and raised his weapon with steady hands. Merle put his fingers in his ears, and John covered his mouth to suppress another laugh, so Mick covered his eyes just to complete the theme. After the first shot was fired, Jefferson frowned, but he fired two more.

"Sir—" he said.

"I know. Didn't even hear any impacts."

Mick twirled in place.

> "The magic maelstrom forms a sphere
> That makes your bullets disappear!"

"Look, give me a chance to talk to her," said Merle. "We, ah, have a history."

"They used to date," said John, and he cracked himself up.

"No, sir," said the staff sergeant. "I can't allow a civilian in there. If we can't neutralize the machine at a distance, then me and my men will have to secure the room."

"I really don't think that's the best idea—"

The younger marines fell into formation around the staff sergeant, and on his signal they rushed into bedlam.

The man on point began almost immediately to float upward into the air—then he turned upside down, then his fatigues turned pink. The marine called Jefferson

dropped his rifle and commenced singing a heartfelt rendition of "La Vie en Rose" in the original French, while another marine nearby kept tripping over thorny vines that sprouted spontaneously through the linoleum. Two more marines were slow dancing, and now the vines were blossoming and actually wrapping their way up several ankles, and soon Merle and Jon and Mick heard an order to retreat and all the men fought their way back into the hall.

Jefferson stared out at nothing in particular. "Don't even *know* French," he whispered.

The staff sergeant was cradling a Dalmatian that he hadn't had when he'd gone into the room.

"Okay," he told Merle. "You have five minutes."

CHAPTER 28

Merle stepped forward, and as soon as he did, the screaming stopped.

"MMMERLIN," said the shining woman in the eye of the storm.

"Hey, honey," said Merle.

The swirling glamour surrounded him now, and his appearance changed. Recently he'd swapped the robe he'd been given in the Village of Reek for more workmanlike clothing in Antarctica, but now these coverings spun outward and wove themselves into a robe again—the robe he'd worn so many centuries ago, actually. The very same. His hat became a skullcap, his shoes soft boots.

Then Nimue clenched her hands, and with some effort the light in her dimmed so that she looked more or less like herself. More or less.

Merle gazed at her poreless smoothness and found himself thinking not the word *skin*, but rather *covering*. She had the look of something flawlessly manufactured. She would come with instructions for care. She would be kept out of direct sun and wiped down occasionally with a damp cloth. She should have looked her most beautiful, but she also looked her least human; and Merle understood that, to his eyes, she couldn't be both.

"I see Sir John," said Nimue. "The leprechaun, Mick— is he with you too?"

Merle glanced over his shoulder. "He's right there. Can't you see him? The little Lord of the Dance?"

Nimue was silent. She looked as if she was about to cry.

"Heh. Heee! She can't see me," said Mick as he turned and reeled. "That's . . . ha! That's her honor, what's left of it."

"What's this?" asked the staff sergeant as he soothed his Dalmatian.

John held his laughter long enough to explain about the honor of the Fay.

"Most fairies," he said, "most fairies think that doing right means doing well. Winning, having more luck and glamour, that sort of thing. If you act honorably, the universe rewards you."

"They've got some weird ideas about right and wrong," said the marine.

"They do," John agreed. "That's true. But deep down, Nimue must know what she's doing is evil."

"That's why she can't see me, I'll reckon," said Mick, suddenly grave. "That's why the glamour hurts her, though it makes the likes o' John an' me delirious. She don't feel she's one o' the Good Folk anymore."

"Look at them back there," said Nimue. "Whispering. Conspiring. You've brought an army, I see. I have an army too."

Merle tilted his head, held his palms out in what he hoped was a nonthreatening way. "Do you, though?" he asked. "Your Freemen have mostly split. And my new friends back there with the fancy cell phones tell me that your block party is breaking up."

Nimue was silent for a moment. "I don't believe you."

"Oh, you know how kids can be. They're all excited for the sleepover until suddenly it's the middle of the night and they all want to go home."

She was glowing fiercer again, and looking more angry than sad.

"They tell me the sky is on fire out there," Merle continued. "The whole thing's out of control. And maybe me and my friends are kinda to blame for that, but you have to end it. You have to end it before there isn't *any* kind of world left for your people."

"Lies."

Merle drew nearer. "It's not lies, and you know it's not. Tell me you can feel it."

"Not a step closer, Merlin. I know your tricks."

"I'm so sorry, honey. I'm sorry about everything. I still don't understand how I split the worlds apart, but believe me that I never meant to. I was just trying to save the world I knew." Merle winced, even as he advanced. Then he sighed, a long, shriving sigh like all his parts were settling inside him. "No. I'm such a liar. I was trying to save my mom and dad. That's all . . . that's all it was ever about, was that. I wanted my mom and dad back."

"I can paralyze you, Merlin. Not another step."

"Oh, please. Look at you. You don't have the fine control for a spell anymore. You can barely keep the rift open. You're not all delicate fingers anymore, sweetheart, you're a big fist. The best you could do is throw a wild punch, and that'd probably kill me, and you've never killed so much as a horsefly without getting a secret cult of Freemen to do it for you."

Still Merle came closer. Only a dozen feet separated them now.

"Just because I don't want to doesn't mean I won't."

Merle considered this.

"No. No, it *doesn't*, does it?"

Mick inhaled sharply. "He's gonna do it."

"Do what?" said John.

"Don't do it, lad! There's gotta be another way!"

But Merle vaulted forward, toward Nimue and the machine. Later (and there would be a later, for some), John would be unable to recollect if it had seemed in slow motion only in his mind or because of Nimue's weird magic. But: to protect her plans, the Godmother lashed out with a fiery haymaker that knocked the old man clean off his feet and backward, somersaulting, crumpling to the ground.

The marines began to move, but Mick held out an arm. "No, no," he said. "Not safe yet."

Nimue looked upon what she had done and wailed. The vortex of witchcraft around her seemed to fly apart, scatter like birds from a dead tree. The magical engine went to pieces with pings and cracks, and the men in the hall had to duck the shrapnel. Then Nimue crawled, as if legless, across the pockmarked floor to where Merle lay.

"Stupid man!" she shouted. "Fool! Oh, my darling."

"No," said John in hushed tones, and he started into the room. "No. She doesn't get to come *near* him." But Mick rushed in and grabbed John around the legs, tackled him. "Mick! What're you doing?"

"I know, son, I'm sorry. But yeh don't wanna get in that one's way just yet."

The storm of glamour had subsided, but Nimue still

crackled and glowed. She was glowing brighter as she clutched at Merle's lifeless body.

"Say something," she told him. "You always thought you were so smart, so clever. Say something smart. Some famous last words."

She pulled herself up to him so that they were almost embracing, like lovers.

"You broke the spell, you villain. Say it. Say 'I told you so.' Say 'I . . . I didn't know you cared.'"

But Merle didn't, couldn't. And Nimue burned whiter and brighter until the light of her consumed them both; and when John and Mick and the rest lowered their hands from their eyes, both witch and wizard were gone.

"Ow," said Emily in the park, and she clutched at her face.

Erno leaned around her. "What's wrong?"

"My headgear just fell out."

The elaborately fashioned metal of it had just unraveled and sprung from her mouth.

"Huh. Well, you didn't need it anyway, right?"

"Kids," said Biggs, pointing. "Sky."

Everyone looked as the fire faded, burned out as if for lack of oxygen. The marines cheered. They could see now that it was early morning—the sun would be up soon.

But there was still a dark scar in the heavens. Emily watched it.

"Young lady," said the queen as the men high-fived all around her. "Is it not over?"

Emily searched her mind. "Nimue's dead," she said. "But it's feeding on itself, now."

John sobbed, sitting awkwardly in an empty spot where his friend had been. Mick put a hand on his shoulder.

"We were always taking the mickey out of each other," said John. "Just teasing, you know? But what if he didn't know I liked him?" He wiped his face. "What . . . what if he didn't like *me*?" he added, as if that wasn't a thought that occurred to him much.

"Yeh've no cause to worry," said Mick. "An elf gets to be my age, an' he sees how people are."

There was a mewing sound, and a plain gray cat approached and rubbed itself from head to tail against John's hip.

"Hullo," John sniffed. "Is this . . . is this the unicat? What was Harvey calling him . . . Grimalkin?"

"Not a unicat no more," said Mick.

John lifted the animal into his lap. "Still a good boy, though."

The staff sergeant drew up alongside them.

"I'm sorry to interrupt your . . . ," he trailed off. "I'm sorry. But I thought you two would want to hear the reports I'm getting from outside."

John smiled wanly up at him. "It's over, isn't it?" And he had a look that said "It has to be. After all that."

"The fire's cleared. There's no one left at that rift business 'cept the cast of *Fantasia*. But the blackness is still in the sky, and the lightning . . ." The staff sergeant rubbed his neck. "And it's getting worse. I think your friend only bought us time. Time for what, I got no idea."

"Hmm," said Mick.

John turned and seized the leprechaun's shoulders. "Mick, before . . . before you said you had an inkling where Scott was going, and what he was doing. Does he know how to fix this?"

Mick nodded slowly. "I've been thinkin' it over. And I think he might, at that. It won't be easy, though, and it will be dangerous."

"Is this your son we're talking about?" asked the marine. "If he had information, he should have shared it with someone with the training to see it through."

"What trainin' would that be? I'll be keepin' my money on Scott Doe."

"Mick," John pleaded. "Mick, what is my boy up to?"

CHAPTER 29

Here's what Scott was up to:

He breathed evenly through his mouth to keep from freaking out, throwing up, and he looked out the big bay door of what Erno would later inform him was a Black Hawk helicopter as it whisked him over the treetops.

It was like being in the stomach of a huge dragonfly, he thought. And then he thought, no, actually—he'd spent a little time inside a stomach once, and this wasn't really like that at all. It was really more like being inside a military helicopter. Scott sat back and adjusted his helmet, which felt huge, which felt like a bucket.

"What's the plan here, buddy?" asked Haskoll. Scott flinched. He'd no idea the ghost had stowed himself on board. "Running away?"

"I'm busy, Haskoll. Why don't you go teach Papa the true meaning of Christmas or something?"

"I ask—and you just tell me if this is a sore subject, big guy—because all the danger seems to be back in Goodborough, with all your friends and loved ones."

"I'm about to try something stupid," Scott told him. "Stupid and so complicated it's giving me a migraine and if any little part of it goes wrong, I die."

"Sweet. Death's not so bad. Me an' you'll hang out more. We'll sneak into movies."

"If you don't mind," Scott told Haskoll, "I'd rather be alone right now."

"Wish I could oblige, sir" came a voice through Scott's bucket of a helmet. "But somebody has to fly the helicopter." He understood after a moment that it was the pilot, speaking to him over a radio.

"Um, yeah. Sorry," said Scott. "I was just talking to myself."

"If you don't mind me saying so, sir, you seem to do that a lot."

Possibly, thought Scott. He couldn't see Haskoll anymore. "Do you know why you're taking me to the Grand Canyon?" he asked the pilot.

"Yes, sir. I am taking you because those are my orders. Any other reason you think I should know about?"

Scott smiled sort of ruefully. "I could tell you, but you wouldn't believe me."

"On a day like this one, I might believe just about anything."

Scott shrugged. Not that the pilot could see him. "You're taking me there because I lost my sister."

"How's that?"

"It's kind of hard to explain."

"Suit yourself. That's the canyon coming up on your right, by the way."

As if Scott needed telling. He marveled at it. He marveled that, despite all the improbable things he'd seen in the last six months, this should still amaze him. The Grand Canyon was a rough Deco metropolis of painted rock cathedrals and sky islands. A red wound in the earth, filled with mountains.

"Park Service has cleared the area, so I'll be able to bring us down right next to the Skywalk."

The Skywalk was as Rudesby had described it—a huge bend of glass and steel that jutted out like a shelf over the rim of the canyon. It glinted in the glare of two nearby spotlights.

They set down beside one of the ends of the horseshoe, and Scott jumped free quickly, ducking under the rotors, and jogged to the rim. He still wore his helmet. He was vaguely aware of a number of distant men and

women—park rangers, maybe, or just spectators who were waiting to see who was so important that he could have the Skywalk all to himself. He had this idea that the pilot, or any of them, might try to stop him if they had too much time to think about what he was doing, so he had to move fast. Still, it took faith to take that first step out onto the glass deck, with only darkness beneath his feet.

The earth trembled, like an earthquake. *Great*, thought Scott. *And I'm standing on a big glass U on the side of a cliff.*

As he walked, he kept his eyes on the sky. It looked strange, in a way he couldn't define. It was going to be on fire soon, but he was going to miss most of that.

The pilot was following him onto the deck. Scott came to a stop at the halfway point, far out over this giant dark nothing, and hoisted his belly up onto the railing so that he could peer below.

"Sir?" said the pilot. "Sir, be careful."

He saw it—a giant shimmering thumbprint, a smear of air just below the northern tip of the Skywalk. A rift.

"Good," he breathed. "Okay." He hurdled up onto the rail, and balanced there.

"Sir! Sir? I need you to get down immediately and step back from the railing!"

"What's about to happen . . . ," Scott told him, "you should know afterward that it wasn't an accident. That I meant to do it, and that you shouldn't feel bad, if it goes wrong."

"Sir, get down now!"

"And if it goes right, then there's about to be an eagle. So watch out for that," Scott added, and jumped.

CHAPTER 30

He didn't remember closing his eyes, but moments later he tumbled into a coarse web of thick ropes and opened them to find himself suspended a dizzying fifty feet over the stone floor below. And on the floor, a dead whale. Something screeched, and he had to give it some thought before deciding that it hadn't been him.

He yanked off his helmet and disentangled his legs, and rolled over in the net to see three pairs of furious eyes staring down at him.

"Eagles," said Haskoll. "Cool. So where are we, that pixie witch's castle?"

Scott scrambled clumsily to the edge of the net as the eagles watched him from their perches above. One of them shifted from side to side on its cartoonishly deadly feet.

"You know," Haskoll said, "last time I saw this place,

there was a bigger-than-average dragon crashing through it. How'd you know it would still be standing?"

"Didn't," said Scott as he found a rolled rope ladder and let it unfurl to the floor. "But Fray did say something about this place being held together by magic."

"Did I?" asked a dry voice. Scott looked about as he descended the ladder and saw the tiny figure of Fray waiting where it touched the floor.

Scott paused, but Fray didn't look like she was out for blood. He finished his descent and stepped gingerly away from the ladder, and the pixie. Behind him was the massive flipper of the poor dead animal that Saxbriton had traded places with only two days before.

"When you and your friends crossed over, you left this behind," said Fray, nodding at the whale. "I've been keeping it for you, in case you came back for it. If you hadn't claimed it in a few days I was going to put up flyers."

"Sorry," said Scott. "Can you maybe just . . . magic it away?"

Fray narrowed her eyes. "I told you once before, I'm—"

"Not a genie, right. Sorry."

Fray tilted her head. "You know what magic is, don't you, boy?"

Scott scanned the great hall of the witch's castle. The huge leaded window was still broken, and a salt wind whipped in and made everything smell like whale. The whale itself nosed out through the ruined window and onto the rocks. Down the north wall, about even with the animal's lifeless eye, Scott could see the rift he thought he wanted.

Fray answered her own question. "It's stubborn belief. It's a tantrum against the universe. You throw your tantrum with such ferocious conviction that the universe breaks down and gives you your candy."

There was also, for some reason, a penguin in here. It skirted the edge of the hall. It had a look of deep loneliness that only solitary penguins in castles can really pull off.

Then Scott heard a rusty metal squeak. A dog and a crew of Fray's ragged humans came up through the floor. Three of them wore only their underwear and confused, panicky expressions. Rudesby waved at him. They were letting him wear pants now.

"Strength of belief has never been a difficulty for me," Fray continued. "It got me cast out of polite society and branded a witch. My Morenwyn believed in the cause of the princes—Denzil's boys—and left with them. What do you believe in, boy?"

"Ghosts," said Haskoll. "Isn't that adorable?"

"I believe . . . ," said Scott, "that you can help me save both of our worlds. Before the elves ruin everything. I'm here for the scabbard."

Fray frowned. "The . . . ," she began, and then her eyes lit. "The *scabbard*. Of course. I've been an idiot. Is it—"

"King Arthur's, yeah," said Scott. "Morgan le Fay stole it from him and threw it into the sea. It must have washed up here. It's probably why there are so many rifts in this place, don't you think? It's warping reality with its magic."

Fray lost herself in thought, muttering and chewing a nail. Her giants shifted uncomfortably in the distance. One of them was wearing a pink rubber helmet, and only then did Scott realize that the three men in their underwear must be Freemen who'd come to Pretannica when Scott, John, and Merle had left it. Maybe the penguin had traded with the queen? Or Mick?

"I have a notion of what you're thinking," said Fray finally. "I wonder if it would have worked. But alas, the thing you seek is currently under three hundred thousand pounds of whale."

Scott turned and winced at the thing. "Oh," he said. "Right." He worked his way, hand over hand, down the side of the animal until he reached the spot where he thought the witch's golden monument might be.

"To answer your question," said Fray, "no. I cannot simply magic this away. It was our intention to begin carving it up and hauling the pieces out to the rocks to feel the gulls—but that will take weeks."

"Haskoll?" said Scott as he searched the chamber for

the ghost. "Are you still here?"

"Up here, buddy! Just messin' with the eagles."

"To whom do you speak, boy?"

"Haskoll . . . you could get that scabbard, couldn't you?"

Haskoll descended slowly, like a leaky balloon. "S'pose I could, champ. Don't want to, though."

"You wouldn't be doing it for me," said Scott, feeling desperate and antsy. "It'll save the whole world! *Two* worlds!"

"I'm dead," said Haskoll. "What do I care about the world?"

"Boy . . . ," said Fray as she peered around the room. "Are you claiming there's a presence here?"

"Lemme guess—you're going to tell me there are no such thing as ghosts now, aren't you?"

"Oh, there are ghosts," said Fray. "After a fashion. But they are exceedingly rare. So many conditions must be met before such a thing can be. Was this Haskoll killed by magic? Did he leave something unfinished? Was he one of the Fay?"

"Um. A pooka made a piece of airplane fall on him, yeah." Scott felt iffy about reminding Haskoll what he'd been in the middle of doing when he died. "And he's a changeling, like me."

"Stop talking about me like I'm not in the room," said Haskoll.

"You aren't in the room," Scott reminded him.

"It isn't his spirit who speaks to you," said Fray. "It's his glamour. The last vestige of it, unleashed onto the world."

"I'm not glamour," said Haskoll, scowling. "I'm me."

"The glamour thinks it's the man. It is animated by the last wish, the thing left undone, the unfinished business. His business is with you, and this is why you see him."

Scott and Haskoll looked at each other. Haskoll drifted a bit closer.

"Well, shoot," he said. "I think I can remember what my business was with Scotty here."

But Scott—Scott thought maybe he understood Haskoll after all. He knew better than to share this with Haskoll, though. The man struck him as the type who didn't want to be understood. Who might do something crazy, just to prove you wrong. But here's what Scott thought: that Haskoll had had every opportunity to kill him, or get him killed, over the past eight days. And he hadn't. He thought he understood Haskoll's unfinished business better than Haskoll.

"Two worlds," Scott said, piercing the hush of the room, barely. "Everyone you've ever known, saved. I just need that scabbard."

Haskoll's face pruned, looked suddenly ghoulish. "Didn't you hear Thumbelina? I'm not . . . I'm not even a proper ghost! When Haskoll was alive, he didn't care about anyone or anything, and I'm less a man than he ever was! I got no stake! None of this is real—it's just some dumb story!"

There was another rumble—through the ground, the air, across every mote of reality.

"So . . . don't you want to know how it ends?" asked Scott.

Haskoll stared at him. And then the whale. He smirked. Then he took and held a deep breath, which probably wasn't strictly necessary, and dove into the whale.

The castle was pretty quiet.

"So," Scott said to Fray after a moment. "Too bad about your window. It was nice."

"Took two weeks of incantations to craft it, and half a second to break." Fray sighed.

"I . . . guess my sister left with Fi and your daughter?"

"She did. I can only tell you that she looked well when she did so."

"Thanks."

Then a spectral arm thrust up out of the top of the whale, out the blowhole, actually, and it was grasping the scabbard of Excalibur. Fray's giants gasped.

"*Da-da-da-daaa,*" sang Haskoll, apparently trying to gild the moment with a little pomp. "*Da-da-da-da-da-daa-da-da-da-da-da-da-da-da-da-da-da-daa-da-da-daaaaa,*" he continued. Maybe the Twentieth Century Fox theme was the only trumpety song Haskoll knew. The ghost emerged entirely from the whale and tossed the scabbard to Scott. Scott fumbled the catch but got it before it hit the floor.

"All right," said Haskoll, "let's see what you do with . . . with it. Hey. Hey, wait." Haskoll's already insubstantial form was beginning to pale. "Are you *kidding me?*"

"This was your unfinished business," said Scott.

"What, going Dumpster diving in a dead whale? *Come on!*"

"Deciding. Deciding whether to help me or hurt me. I remember that night in the park, looking down the barrel of your gun while you made speeches. Talking, talking, talking. Stalling for time while you decided whether you could really shoot an unarmed eleven-year-old in the chest. And all this past week—just watching, never acting. Because you didn't know who you were."

"Not true," said Haskoll, or the barest wisp of Haskoll. "Not true. I'm cold-blooded. I could have killed you. I *still* can."

And the ghost rushed Scott, bleeding glamour, losing shape, until it flew apart just inches from his face and faded back into the ether.

"He's left this world, hasn't he?" asked Fray.

"Yes," said Scott. "I mean, I think so."

"How odd. I could not feel him till I felt his passing. Like a ringing in the ear, heard only in its sudden absence."

"Okay. Which one of these rifts goes to the ocean?"

Fray jerked her head. "The ocean? Surely not. I have a rift that can take you to your home in England, if I shrink you first."

Scott shook his head and thought of his friends, and his father. "My home is in New Jersey. Currently. Please—the ocean rift. I kinda sorta know what I'm doing."

Fray shrugged theatrically and waved her hand at a low stall near the ruined window. "*Mea octagon est vestra octagon,*" she muttered.

It was a small stall, with an oily octagon barely bigger than a stop sign. So Scott dropped into a squat, curled himself into the rift, and waited. The scabbard dug into his armpit like a crutch. But not like a metal crutch—it was inexplicably warm.

He took a deep breath and held it, waiting for the ocean to swallow him. Fray appeared near his shoulder.

"I feel like I ought to offer you something," she said. "Cup of tea? Water? You might be here for some time."

Scott shook his head and tried to smile in a friendly way, which was hard to reconcile with his puffed cheeks and little ziplocked mouth.

"You know," Fray continued, "if that really is the

scabbard of Excalibur you're clutching, then I wonder if you need to breathe at all. There's an interesting thought. Are you accustomed to holding your wind this long?"

Scott was about to agree that yes, he *had* been holding it awhile, hadn't he, when he was suddenly struck by the feeling that he was sharing interdimensional space with a giant fish. Which is a hard feeling to describe. Like love, you just know it when you're in it.

Then the ocean was all around, and Scott hadn't the chance to tell Fray thank you, nor say good-bye, nor hear the witch announce over the wet flopping body of Scott's replacement that they'd be having tuna tonight.

CHAPTER 31

The middle of the Atlantic Ocean was frigid and dark. Scott tumbled in the water, feeling the brush of smaller fish against his skin and a cold ache in his eyes. His ears opened and closed. Then, panic—he didn't know which way was up. In his fright he gave a shout that bubbled out and away from him. There. Follow the bubbles. He let the rest of his breath go and trailed the dotted line of it to the surface.

When he breached and gasped for breath, he gasped for breath because it seemed like the thing to do—though his lungs felt fine, really. He swiveled in the water, looking around him. The sky was dark and gray above, with a light rain whipped into mist by a fitful wind that made the ocean choppy. There was no land, nothing to be seen in any direction. No, that wasn't true—there was a little wedge of something cresting the waves to his right. A gray, triangular something. A fin.

"Oh, come on," Scott whispered. He thrashed his arm through the water and reached for the merrow's cap in his back pocket.

The fin had disappeared and then reappeared again about thirty feet to his left.

He was nearly positive that he'd put the cap in one of his back pockets, but he went ahead and checked his front pockets anyway.

"No no no no no," he said, and scanned the wavelets for a glimpse of red. Then he dunked his head and was treated to a good face-to-face look at the great white shark that was stalking him—fifteen feet of sleek gray fighter jet with a dead black pit of an eye and a humorless grin. A "why are you hitting yourself?" kind of grin.

Then, just past the shark, Scott spotted the cap. The red of it was nearly black in the water, slipping listlessly along just below the surface. He tucked the scabbard down his shirtfront and kicked under the shark's tail as it passed. He supposed that nothing good would come of taking his eyes off the cap, even for a moment, so he wasn't watching the shark as it turned and hurtled suddenly toward him like it had finally decided what it wanted for dinner.

Scott reached for the cap, too soon, and actually swept it a little farther out of his grasp. *If the shark bites my leg off,* he thought, *at least I won't bleed—the scabbard won't let me. Not to mention the world's ending, so no use crying over eaten legs,* he added as he kicked one last time, and grabbed the hat, and pinwheeled around to see the shark's nightmare face barreling down on him. A child's drawing of a monster, with a great circular mouth and triangle teeth. Scott jammed the hat on his head, thought, *The rift at the bottom of the ocean,* and the beast's jaws snapped shut. But Scott wasn't where he had been.

He dove, spinning, plummeting faster, the water growing darker all around him. After a while he wondered why he was still alive—he hadn't taken a breath in over two minutes. He hadn't noticed that the scabbard was oxygenating his cells for him. *Something* had to, after his heart had stopped and his blood had turned to sap inside him. Arthur had never noticed any of this either, because it turns out it's hard to convince a body not to keep pumping air like the machine it is. But through force of will Scott relaxed his chest and emptied his lungs, and in the starless space at the bottom of the sea his body felt heavy and at rest for the first time all year. The scabbard pressed into his chest, warm as a heart.

Only after he slowed and stopped did Scott realize he'd closed his eyes. So now he opened them and could see the thin plane of another octagonal rift all around him. Even here in the dark, he could see it. And he barely

had a moment to think about that when the wraith of some new animal passed through him and he found himself blinking in a cow pasture in Pretannica.

Pretannica was darker than he remembered. But the grass was still dense and lush and as green as a traffic light. He clutched at it, dripping salt water, and got to his feet. The other cows were looking at him.

"You're staring like you're probably wondering what happened to the cow that was just here," he told them. "I don't really have any good news for you."

"Never had a cow turn into a boy before," someone answered, and for a moment Scott thought one of the animals might be talking to him. He'd seen stranger things lately. But it was a girl about his age, slightly taller. "Once in a while this pasture turns a cow into a big fish, or an octopus. Never a boy." She smoothed her clothes and seemed to flush dimly in the twilight.

"Oh. Hi, maybe you can help me," said Scott. "I'm in a really big hurry. Have you seen, like, a whole lot of elves all marching in the same direction recently? Or something?"

The girl stepped toward him. "I bet you're a prince. Are you? I always expected something like this would happen to me sooner or later."

"What? No. Please, do you know where the elves are?"

"Why would you want to know?"

"I need to find them. All the Fay should be heading for

the same spot, and I need to get there too."

"You can't leave," the girl said. She came close enough to sniff him. "You're mine. I traded Harold Cryer three goats for you."

Something like pink lightning split the sky. Every blade of grass quivered in the thunder that followed.

The girl squinted at the clouds. "What's going on, cow?" she asked him. A fitful wind whipped her hair in every direction. "I haven't never seen a day like today."

"Look," Scott said. He backed away, but the girl kept pace. "I'm sorry, but your cow didn't turn into me. I traded places with your cow. Your cow is at the bottom of the ocean."

One of the herd mooed. "Ohhhhhh," she mooed, like she should've guessed the ocean, like she would've gotten it herself if she'd had another minute to think about it.

"What's an ocean?" asked the girl.

"I don't have time. I'm sorry. Have you heard anything about the elves?"

The girl nodded at something over Scott's shoulder. "Word around town is they're all trooping toward London. But London's no place for a cow."

"Thanks!" Scott called as he ran off. "Sorry again!"

He was barely a mile into the forest before he began to get antsy. How long had it been since he'd left the Grand

Canyon? An hour, maybe? Two? How much time did the world have left? Reality was being made to swallow something impossible, and it rumbled again in its guts. The colossal trees shivered. The leaves above crackled like burned skin and molted free of their canopies. A dark scar was twisting its way across the sky.

He paused on a stump, panting. So much of his plan was just stupid. He hadn't even known the scabbard would save him from drowning. He just thought the ocean floor would be a lot closer than it had been. And now he was running like an idiot with barely an idea where he was going. What he needed, he decided, was to climb up high and have a look around.

There was a tree nearby with so many climbable limbs it almost seemed like a trap. He kicked it a couple times around the base just to see if it would kick back. Of course, the trees might just be trees now—magic was leaving this place through a hole in the universe.

He started climbing, making a spiral ascent up the trunk until the lightning flashed again and he had to cling motionless to a branch and wait out the thunder. Then upward again as the limbs narrowed and his face was raked by twigs and dying leaves, and finally his head breached the top of the canopy to the open sky, and he was immediately slapped in the head by something flimsy and dark.

"Wh . . . hey!" he said to the flimsy slapping thing, and he turned to see that it had only been the wingtip of a passing raven. A colossally monstrous raven. "Waitaminute," he murmured, and swiveled his head to see a second colossally monstrous raven swooping down on him.

CHAPTER 32

"AAAAA!"

"CAAAAW!" the raven answered with its colossally monstrous beak, the same beak that would, in an instant, separate Scott's head from the rest of him if he didn't duck below the safety of the leaves. He crouched fast—too fast—and lost his footing, snapping branches as he dropped ten feet and finally caught a stout branch with the crook of his elbow.

He paused. He had cuts all over him. None of them bleeding, though. He patted the scabbard under his jacket. Then he realized he was missing an opportunity, and he scrambled to the top of the tree again. The canopy swayed as another raven passed overhead. Scott prayed there'd be another as he popped his head above the tree line.

There *was* another raven, the last of the flock, it seemed, a short distance away. Scott waved his arm around and tried to put on an appetizing expression, which in the heat of the moment turned out to be sort of a puckery kissy face. But whatever, it worked. The raven dived and Scott tensed his legs, waiting for the right moment.

The bird was so close now it blotted out the sky, and Scott ducked, felt the horny beak graze his cowlick, and hooked his arm around a leg. He was yanked at once from the tree in a burst of leaves and twigs, and jostled as the raven attempted to hover in place and nip at his face. It loosed a greasy stool and a tuft of feathers.

"Ugh. Just . . . just keep flying!" Scott told it. "Ignore me!"

The talon of the leg he was holding snicked and snapped below him, tearing his jeans and nicking his legs.

"WRAAAAK!"

The raven's cry was faintly answered by several others farther on. Finally the pull of the magic castle or the prospect of losing its flock became too much for it to bear, and the raven continued after the others with Scott in tow.

He could not believe how much his arms were hurting already. And was the bird crapping again? It seemed to be crapping more than the normal amount of crap. The stuff was just narrowly missing Scott's shoes.

"Please stop," he said.

"CAWK," the bird answered.

The raven kept the others in sight but couldn't gain

any ground. Scott switched arms and squinted against the cold air. Tears were streaming down his face, and when he coughed he accidentally swallowed a bug. He felt sorry for himself—just for a moment, just for fun—and that moment was like a warm blanket over his aching shoulders. If his plan worked he'd be a hero, and no one would know how much he'd suffered for them. No one had ever suffered so much.

His reverie was interrupted by a couple of details that suddenly came to mind. Things he'd seen for just an instant as the raven had nearly decapitated him—a certain notch in its beak, a patch of missing feathers around the left eye. This was the same raven that had swallowed and later thrown him up a couple of weeks ago. He was almost sure of it. To the raven, Scott wasn't a hero but rather some horrible kid who kept pranking him like a jerk.

Now they were descending, and banking to follow the snaking course of a wide river below them. Scott supposed it must be the Thames, which ran straight through London, and then it struck him—the Tower of London used to rest permanently on the bank of the Thames before Morgan le Fay magicked it up. It probably returned there whenever Titania wanted to visit the city.

"Thanks for the ride," Scott shouted hoarsely into the wind. "Again. And, um. Sorry." Then, when the bird had descended as low as it seemed inclined to, Scott let go of its leg.

It was still a long drop to the river. Long enough to have time to think about what a long drop it was. He clutched the scabbard and the merrow's cap and hit the water harder than he expected. A few seconds later he was underwater, and he realized he had blacked out.

That's no good, he thought. His arms felt numb. With some effort he slipped the cap over his head and added, *Take me to the elves.* And was whisked five miles down the river in a spray of foam.

Too late he realized that what he should have thought was "Take me *near* the elves," as the magic of the cap, unable to get him all the way by water, just skidded him up an embankment.

"Ow."

He got shakily to his feet. From a great distance came the sound of drums. The London of Pretannica was a much smaller city than the London he knew, and it huddled behind a Roman wall. Here, outside the wall, it was barely more than fields and cobblestone roads. Scott stumbled up one of these roads toward the drums, which, as he drew closer, were joined by flutes and fiddles and fifes. All of which were drowned out momentarily by a bone-shaking thunder. The Fay were having an end-of-the-world party, and Scott was the party pooper.

Before he saw the elves, he saw humans—hundreds atop tall rocks, huddled in trees with spyglasses, or just milling on the ground below.

"Boy," an old woman said to him, "you're hurt." Her face was aghast—did he really look that bad?

"I'm . . . fine," Scott answered. "Just some scrapes." All the men and women and children in the trees were focused on some distant spot he couldn't see. The elves, he figured. The rift.

"Your wounds are fresh, but they do not bleed," the woman told him.

Scott felt like a change of subject. "I just got here. What are the elves doing?"

The woman wrung her hands and winced at the horizon. "They're all there. *All* of them, and certain beasts as well. My daughter tells me that they walk beneath an arch of roses that wasn't there yesterday. She says that when they walk beneath the arch they change into children. If we come any closer, the elves shoot arrows at our feet."

Scott found himself wanting to comfort her. "It'll all be over soon," he said, even as the sky darkened above him. "And then it's gonna be great. I promise." He started to move toward the crowd.

"How do you know?" called the woman.

That was a good question. "I'm . . . from the future," Scott lied.

The woman turned her eyes toward the sky. "I don't think there's any such thing," she said.

Scott moved through the people, who for the most part were too preoccupied with anxious gossip to pay him any attention. But occasionally someone, usually a child, would look his way and gasp. Soon both the crowd and the trees thinned, and someone grabbed his shoulder.

"Ow," said Scott.

The man grimaced at him. "Boy, you look—"

"Great, right? I feel great. What do you want?"

The man blinked. "Only to tell you . . . to tell you not to step into the clearing. It isn't safe."

It wasn't a natural clearing. A thousand trees lay felled on the ground. The elves had cut a path for themselves to the rift. He could see the throng of them now: Fay of every size and description, trailing banners and garlands of flowers and ivy. Playing instruments and making merry even as the sky opened like a great black mouth above them. They faced a large arch of rose vines that reminded Scott of the steps he'd once climbed into Titania's court. Titania herself oversaw the festivities from atop a pillowed sedan chair held aloft by her giants, while griffins and birds and even a Pegasus gyred above.

The rift itself was contained inside the rose arch, as wide as a Ferris wheel. Did the elves see the way its edges trembled? No, of course not—they couldn't see it at all. And as Scott watched, the rift actually grew *larger*. It was out of control, feeding on glamour. So. This was the way the worlds ended—swallowed by an oily hole in reality.

Already a thousand children or more had made the Crossing from Goodborough and were marching with lifeless eyes from the rose arch to the opposite end of the clearing.

"Okay, good tip," Scott said to the man. "Thank you. I'll have to be sneaky, then."

"What do you mean?"

Before the man could stop him, Scott crouched low and darted into the clearing, up to the nearest fallen tree trunk, then along that to the next trunk, always keeping out of sight, always—

There was an arrow in Scott's foot. He hadn't even felt it land. But he felt it now like an electric pounding drumbeat up his left leg. He dropped to the ground.

"OW! JEEZ!"

The clearing got dead quiet. A lyrical voice turned like a music box in his mind:

> *"I trust my shining eyes be not deceived?*
> *It seems young Scott hath got himself mischieved."*

"I'M TRYING TO SAVE YOU!" Scott called across the clearing. "OKAY? I'M TRYING TO SAVE EVERYONE, FAY AND HUMAN!"

"You had your day in court—you pled your suit.
We listened to your point and found it moot.
I trust you see our own has pierced thine boot."

"OH, *COME ON!* YOUR *POINT* PIERCED MY *BOOT?* THAT'S NOT SHAKESPEARE, THAT'S LIKE BAD ACTION MOVIE DIALOGUE."

Titania was silent for a moment.

"The Scottish Doe of old was ne'er so bold."

"YEAH, WELL, I'VE HAD A REALLY BAD DAY."

Tall elves wended their way through the felled tree trunks toward him. They carried long pole weapons topped with jagged arrays of hooks and spikes like huge keys—keys that could open any part of Scott they liked.

With a wave from Titania, the drums and fiddles started up again. Like she wanted Scott to know that he was such small potatoes she wasn't even going to turn down her music.

He tried to think of how to explain himself. To explain that the sword Excalibur and its scabbard were linked by the spell that had created them—one to cleave and the other to protect. They were bound together like the Tower and its ravens. Some story should have reunited them, eventually.

320

But then Arthur left in a time machine, carrying the sword. Sword tried to cleave its way into a new future, but the spell that bound it wouldn't let it leave scabbard behind. Arthur got trapped in between, unable to come through to Goodborough, where Merle waited. But with the stolen power of the time machine, the sword cut reality in twain, a sharp spike through two overlapping worlds—even as the scabbard drew the world's magic close and protected what was left.

So a bubble of magic, protected by a lost scabbard. And a king with a sword, forever trying to cut his way free. Bring the scabbard to Earth, and the sword can finally follow, and all would be reunited. He figured.

It felt like a lot to have to shout across a field.

Then there was a poleax in his face.

"Rise," said an elf, "so that we may bind thy wrists, and take thee to thy judgment at the feet of fair—"

A rock bounced off the elf's helmet.

He turned, furious. Nearby, the other elves crouched into defensive positions. "Who dares?" he cried.

A man, the same man Scott had spoken to right before getting shot in the foot, stepped out from the darkness of the trees. "Lea—leave him alone!" he said, barely shouting, his voice a warble. "He's just a boy!"

Another rock sailed out and missed the elves entirely. It hadn't been thrown by the man, however—a fact that was not lost on anyone.

"Return to your homes!" called the elf. "This does not concern you!"

More rocks now, many of which were landing dangerously close to Scott himself, not that he didn't appreciate the sentiment. The elves were joined by more and more compatriots with spears and swords, yet the humans too emerged from hiding in greater numbers. Scott noted grimly that few were armed against the elves with anything worse than sticks and stones. Sticks and stones wouldn't break their bones. This was a time for words.

"Fairies of Oberon!" shouted the same elf. "Fall in line!" And the army of Titania formed rows as best they could amid the fallen trees.

"No!" said Scott. "Please, don't hurt them!" He turned to face the people. "Get back! Back into the forest! I'll be fine!"

"Fairies of Oberon! Charge!"

"BUG ZAPPERRRR!" answered a chorus of voices nearby, and a string of birds swooped low and crossed the paths of the advancing Fay. The bird in the lead breathed blue fire. The next four carried pixies. Astride the last was Polly.

The fire startled everyone, Scott included. That, plus a family of pixies flying past their ankles, had a profound effect on the regiment of elves. They tripped over tree trunks, branches, their own feet. They inadvertently stabbed their toes and the toes of others. Whole teeming companies of elves tumbled over, only to trip up the row immediately behind them.

"PIXIE JINX!" called Polly, and she flew to Scott's shoulder on the back of a starling as he got to his feet. "You came back," she said. "Did you forget something?"

He smiled at her. "You know I did."

"I'm trying not to tell you how horrible you look. But it's really superscary."

"I'll be all right," Scott told her, though he wasn't sure. "I just have to get through that rift."

Finchbriton was setting trunks alight, keeping the elves off balance. The people by the trees continued to throw rocks, and now the trooping Fay seemed uncertain what to do.

"I have this scabbard under my shirt," said Scott.

"This what?" said Polly. The starling whistled something anxiously, and Polly whistled back. This seemed to calm it.

"Scabbard. A sheath, like for a sword. It's a long story, so you'll have to trust me. You need to take the scabbard and fly to the rift. Once you go across, you have to take it to that big park Mom took us to that day, do you remember?"

"I can't carry that," said Polly. "It's too big."

"Please try. I'll . . . I don't know. Distract Titania and

323

the others while you do it."

They were nearing Titania's royal retinue and the long line of Fay and magical beasts waiting to make the Crossing. Scott was still trying to be sneaky, but he was pretty sure they were all watching him. He crouched behind a tangled trunk.

Some of the children of Goodborough still mingled near the rose arch where they'd come across. But they now appeared to be waking as if from a very deep sleep. They began to wander, unbidden. More than one called for his mother.

Fi and Morenwyn, astride a crow, landed on Scott's opposite shoulder.

"What cheer, Scott," said Fi. "You look abysmal."

"Thanks."

"I'm supposed to take this scabby thing through the rift," Polly told them.

Fi eyed Scott's many injuries. "That's not a fair thing to call your brother," he said.

"Scabbard," Scott said, and he showed them. "Not scab, scabbard. I have the scabbard of Excalibur."

Morenwyn gasped. "Mother's monument. How did you—?"

"She let me take it," Scott told her. "After I told her what it was. Honest."

"You may trust in Scott, my dear," said Fi.

"Well . . . if that is the scabbard of Excalibur," said Morenwyn to Polly, "then it's the only thing keeping your brother alive."

Titania asked a dog-headed aide,

> *"What fresh iniquity is this he plans*
> *With yon antiquity, which by his hands*
> *Hath risen from the sea to grace my lands?"*

but you could tell she wanted Scott to hear her.

"I didn't follow that one," Scott admitted.

"She wants to know what the scabbard's for," said Fi.

Just then the sky erupted in pink flame. A stirring vortex of it began to sink into a funnel that seemed to be lowering its blazing finger down on everyone in the clearing. Human and Fay alike cried out, and put down their weapons, and gaped. Again the music stopped, and it was suddenly very quiet. Until Titania cried out.

> *"No rarer mortal wound was ever scored*
> *Than that which comes by scabbard, not by sword!*
> *Oh, fie! What power hath this cursed gift*
> *Which lights the sky but douses out our rift?"*

"What?" said Scott. "I'm not doing this! What about your rift?"

"Scott," said Fi. "Are you certain your scabbard is not the cause?"

"Yeah. Why?"

"We were watching the rift for a while before you got here," said Polly. "And it's like it stopped working right after you arrived. Haven't you noticed? Nobody's left and no kids have come through for a while now."

"But it's still there," said Scott. "It's getting bigger, even."

"I see it too," said Polly. "But they don't."

The dog-headed aide stepped forward with an announcement.

> *"By order of Titania the first:*
> *Destroy the boy and break apart his prize*
> *And stone his bones and take his heart and eyes;*
> *The best reward to he who does the worst."*

"Jeez," said Polly.

All the pixies were here now—Denzil and Fee and Fo rallied around—and Finchbriton came to rest on Scott's head. Scott was covered in birds and tiny people.

"It would have worked." Scott sighed. "My plan. I swear it would have."

"I believe you," said Polly.

Every kind of elf and beast descended on them.

CHAPTER 33

"HALT!"

It was Titania who had spoken. At least, Scott *thought* it was Titania—it sounded a little panicky for her. And it hadn't even rhymed with anything.

The approaching swarm of blade and hoof and talon and claw *did* halt, and then they all looked back to see the changeling Dhanu standing behind Queen Titania with a blade at her throat. He spoke.

> *"Make way, and let the boy and pixies pass,*
> *Lest wicked fate befall this stately head*
> *And terminate this once great head of state."*

"Good one," said Fo.

"I thought it was forced," said Fee.

The crowd parted, and Scott passed elf and glittering

sprite, griffin and manticore, giant and ogre and troll. Also shimmering moths, a family of trees, a golem twisted out of intricate wire, a woman made of bees.

"It's so quiet," said Scott. He could hear the crunch of the grass beneath his feet. "There's nothing as quiet as a crowd of people staring at you and not saying anything."

"Unless maybe a crowd of monsters staring at you and not saying anything," Polly offered.

Soon he stood once more before the High Queen of the Seelie Court, Titania of the Fay. The giants holding her sedan chair aloft were looking abashed and self-conscious. Dhanu must have leaped onto the back of the chair from a nearby tree. His hand, the hand holding the knife, was trembling. Titania herself appeared smaller than she had in the Tower, smaller even than she'd looked only twenty minutes ago. She might have been Scott's age. She said,

"My changeling friend would never be so brash—"

but Dhanu wouldn't let her finish even a stanza. He pressed the quivering knife closer.

"My faithless queen will keep her tongue in check.
A hunted life has made me passing brash."

330

"Dhanu," said Scott. "Thank you. You've been a good friend. But I don't want to do it like this."

Dhanu looked doubtful.

"Careful, Scott," whispered Fi. "Loathsome as it may be, we have to press every advantage."

"No, Scott's right," said Polly. "Look at her—she's just a kid."

"She's as ageless as stone, little sister."

"Please," said Scott. "You put the knife down, and I'll walk over to that rift, and Her Majesty won't stop me because . . . because she'll look into my heart or whatever and know I'm not up to anything. And tomorrow we'll think about all the mistakes we almost made."

Dhanu looked rattled. But he slowly lowered his blade.

"For good or grievous ill, I'll trust in Scott."

Only when the danger was past did Titania shiver. She breathed greedily, and swelled a bit with each inhalation, and looked to be about to speak but checked herself.

Scott walked swiftly to the rose arch before anyone changed their mind. He looked about him and saw a hundred thousand humans and Fay watching his every move. A single baby was crying somewhere. Fifty or so Goodborough kids lingered near the rift, looking shell-shocked. Scott thought he recognized one of them.

"You're that new kid," said Denton Peters. "Aren't you? You were the one in the bus station bathroom who thought elves were stealing his backpack."

"It was a leprechaun," Scott answered, walking past. "We're friends now."

"I'd forgotten about you, but . . . you haven't been in school since Erno and Emily disappeared, have you?"

"I've been busy with stuff. Can we catch up later, Denton? I'm kind of in the middle of something."

"Uh, yeah. Sure. Sorry."

Scott stopped at the threshold of the huge arch. It wasn't so quiet anymore—the furnace in the sky roared, and the fiery tornado it was forming had nearly touched down.

"This is it," Scott said to Polly. "Take the scabbard."

No," said Polly. "I won't. Morenwyn says it's keeping you alive."

"Polly, please. I came back here to save you. Let me save you."

"You're not just saving me, you're saving everybody."

Scott winced. "I know. But it was easier to think about if it was just you."

Polly urged her bird away, and then so did the pixies. "Go," she said. "I don't understand what you're doing, but I'm sure it'll work. I'll see you in a few minutes."

Scott almost broke down. But he forced himself into the rift.

"I keep leaving people," he whispered.

After a few moments in the rift, he wondered if his plan was doomed to fail after all.

Titania said,

> "Alas, at last you find your hopes denied—
> There's no one waiting on the other side."

But then Scott was gone.

CHAPTER 34

And he was back in Goodborough.

Mick was waiting there for him, and the leprechaun shied at the sight of Scott's injuries.

"Lad—"

"I know. Forget it. Who traded places with me?"

Mick smiled. "Who d' yeh think?"

Dad, thought Scott, his eyes stinging. *Of course Dad.* He blinked until he could see clearly again.

"We have to get—"

"To the park, I know it," said Mick. He waved at a nearby jeep. "Meet our new friend the staff sergeant— he's gonna give us a ride."

The sky was on fire again here too.

Scott and Mick piled into the jeep. "Is that the unicat?" asked Scott.

The jeep peeled out.

"Essentially," said Mick. "An' Emily an' Erno an' Biggsie are okay. They're here."

Scott breathed. Even though he didn't really need to.

"So is everyone waiting at the park?"

Mick didn't answer right away. "Almost everyone," he said.

The jeep bucked right up into the park and skidded to a halt next to a cluster of people.

"Scott!" Emily sang. "Omigosh!" She ran to hug him, then seemed to reconsider at the last moment. "You look like garbage. Do you really have it?"

Scott showed her the scabbard. It felt strange, like it was dragging something behind him, like it was getting more and more massive with each step. Eventually he had no choice but to drop it, and it landed like a monument in the center of Merle's octagonal ring.

Emily leaned in, and breathed. She squeezed her eyes tight, concentrating, and a beautiful pinkness flowed out of her.

Then everyone, Scott and Mick and Emily and Erno and Biggs and the queen and the United States Marines were knocked backward, and when they raised their heads there was an old but magnificent man standing in the center of it all. He wore a crown, and armor, and had a horrible wound in his side. He looked down.

"Oh. *There* it is," he said, and with some effort he retrieved the scabbard from the ground and sheathed his sword. Then he looked around at the unlikely group of people surrounding him. "What's all this, then?"

Scott turned to face him. "You're the once and future king, returned to save us in our time of greatest need," he wheezed. "Also, I helped." Then he collapsed.

Blood rushed now from his injuries, as if to make up for being late. Above him, the sky was clearing. The worlds were blithely merging. Emily leaned over him.

He smiled at her. She couldn't smile back. "Big magical hoo-ha," he told her as she pressed on his wounds.

King Arthur was already being tended to by the marines, and the queen. He turned his head this way and that.

"Where's Merlin?" he asked.

COMMERCIAL BREAK

EPILOGUE

Emily and Erno and Biggs stood in front of a narrow little house in Brooklyn. Biggs was freshly shaved and looked nice in his custom suit and tie. Erno looked rumpled as usual. Emily looked as radiant as she ever had, and was even wearing her hair up for the first time. She'd grown an inch in the last month.

A little winged fairy flitted overhead. A car passed in the street behind. Erno checked the address again.

"It's right," said Emily.

"This is weird," Erno said.

"You said so on the train. I agreed."

"Okay," Erno breathed. "Let's do it, I guess."

They were about to step forward when Biggs stopped them.

"Kids," he said. "Harvey."

The rabbit-man was standing in the next little yard,

half covered by bushes. But he was visible. He was wearing his glamour. And the fact that a passing cyclist only gave the rabbit-man a brief glance, like you might give a clown or a person on crutches, showed just how much the world had changed in five weeks.

Harvey stepped out. Biggs growled.

"What are *you* doing here?" said Emily. She might have growled a little too.

"Tying up loothe endth," said Harvey. He offered them a photograph in his outstretched hand. Emily glared at him, but took it.

It was a picture of Mr. Wilson. A new picture. He looked as old as ever, but his hair was trimmed shorter than the twins had ever seen it and his mustache was gone.

"He's okay?" Emily gasped. "Where is he?"

"In an athithted living home in Delaware. He doethn't remember anything from the latht year, or claimth not to. But he'th doing better. I've written the addreth on the back. If you wanna vithit him, you'd better thoon. They're gonna let him move out."

Emily smiled. But it was the mild smile, Erno noted, of someone who was merely pleased that an old friend was doing okay. "We never knew what happened to him," she told Harvey. "He just took off again, the morning of the Merging. We were beginning to fear the worst."

Unseen by Emily, Erno and Biggs shared a look.

"*Really*," said Harvey. "Well. Theemth he fell off a bridge and landed right in my rowboat."

Erno frowned. "You were there? What were you doing in a rowboat?"

Harvey spat. "Coming back to *help*," he said, and he screwed up his face like the thought disgusted him. "Can you believe it? I'd thpent tho much time around Mick, I'd thtarted developing a conscience. Ain't never had one of thothe before."

Emily whispered, "Fell off a bridge—"

"But now he's fine," Erno interrupted.

"Sure. Jutht tell yourthelf it wath all a dream," Harvey said, and he turned to leave. "Don't follow me, any of you," he added. "Don't try to get in touch. You and me? We're done. I never want to thee you people again for the retht of my life, and that'th gonna be a long time. Elth the Puck a liar call."

And he walked off down the street toward the train station without a second glance.

"See ya, Harvey!" said Erno. "Stay sweet."

Emily handed the photo to Biggs, because she didn't have any pockets. She sighed.

"So do you . . . ," Erno began. "Do you want to visit him?"

"Mr. Wilson?" Emily thought. "Why don't we let him

come to us?" she said finally.

"Yeah."

They walked up the path to the Brooklyn house.

"Should I knock?" said Emily. "Maybe I shouldn't ring the bell—I don't want to wake him."

Erno went ahead and knocked while she thought about it.

A young woman with curly brown hair opened the door and flinched at the sight of them. But she recovered quickly—she probably just mistook Biggs for an actual giant.

"Yes? Hi. Are you . . . are you here for the bris?"

"What's a bris?" asked Erno.

"Um, sure," said Emily. "Yes. We're here for the bris."

The woman glanced at Biggs again. "Are you friends of my husband's?"

"We're friends of Merle's," Emily told her with a smile.

Ms. Lynn laughed. "Merle is eight days old. He doesn't have any friends." They stared at one another for a moment. Then the woman stepped aside. "Well, whatever. You're welcome. Little Merle is in the first room on the right."

They walked into the dim hall and turned into a room filled with friends and family. Biggs ducked and tried to keep out of everyone's way. But the kids stepped up to a tiny red baby resting atop a white pouf in a bassinet. He wore thin little mittens over his hands. He also wore a look of deep concentration on his face, this baby, as if he were really considering something. Déjà vu, maybe.

"Hi, Merle," said Emily.

"Merlin," said Erno.

The baby waggled his mittens.

Everyone else in the room had gone quiet, like they could tell something momentous was happening. Or maybe they just recognized the kids and their nanny from television. The Utzes had tried to keep their faces out of the news, but they found that was like trying to uncrack an egg. So they were attempting to make a modest little omelet out of things.

"So," said Emily. "Here's what's been going on. King Arthur and Elizabeth have been really good advocates for the Fay, and so far people have been adjusting pretty well. Nobody's trying to conquer anybody. There's been, you know, skirmishes and things. But humanity seems mostly excited, you know? Like they'd been waiting for something like this to happen."

"You can thank Hollywood for that," said Erno.

"Yeah, and books. Seems like every other book has some kind of magic-is-real theme, right? It's like we've been preparing."

"Scott's been really popular," said Erno with a smirk.

"Like, he's doing talk shows and stuff."

"He pretends to hate the attention," Emily droned. "But you can see him starting to enjoy it a little."

"I saw him on the cover of a magazine called *Teen Fever* the other day. He still looks pretty beat up, but I guess girls like scars."

"Plus the mark."

"Oh right. Titania feels so bad now about how she treated Scott that she marked him with this little glowing moon and star on his forehead. She didn't even ask or anything, she just did it."

"The mark tells all Fay that no one's to mess with Scott unless they want to mess with Titania too. So I guess her heart was in the right place."

"I guess."

They shared a quiet moment. The baby gurgled.

A moment later a man joined them. He almost looked like a younger, more slender Merle, with a trim black beard. Merle's father.

"Excuse me," he said. "Kids? We, uh, don't really understand why you're here. But we're glad! And honored. Um." He looked at something over their heads. "Thing is, we wondered if you might know anything about . . . that." Then he nodded.

Erno and Emily followed his gaze, and jumped. They'd totally missed the white barn owl on the mantle.

"It flew in a few days ago when I went out for diapers," said Mr. Lynn. "It won't leave."

In the Philadelphia airport, some months later, Scott and John and Mick stood in Terminal C and waited. Polly (still winged, still only inches tall) stood atop Scott's shoulder. She examined his face.

"You look tired," she said. "I thought you said you were sleeping better."

Scott tapped the glowing mark on his head. "I have been, ever since I started wearing a headband to bed. But last night I was too . . . you know, excited."

Polly grinned. "Yeah, me too."

John bounced on his toes. "I still think we ought to hide you at first," he told Polly. "Your mum has no idea what's gone on in the past year. I can't imagine what this is going to be like for her."

"She's a tough one," said Mick. "She can take it."

It was nice of the authorities to shut down this terminal for the day. They'd have some privacy when she returned. Scott and Polly's mom, back from the future. Safe.

It was quiet. They didn't really know exactly when she'd be back, but it would be soon.

"I thought Fi was supposed to join us today," John said vaguely.

"No, remember?" said Polly. "Emily told Morenwyn that Emily and Erno and Biggs weren't coming 'cause they thought it should just be for family, so then Morenwyn told Fi, and Fi and Morenwyn decided they should just meet Mom later."

Mick frowned up at her. "So what I am doin' here, then?"

Polly blew a raspberry. "Gimme a break. You're family."

Scott tried to tune them all out and focus on the spot where his mother had disappeared. Where she'd reappear again, more or less. Dad was right—he had so much to tell her. To pass the time, he counted down from ten, as if that made any sense, as if she'd just be there when he finished. And even as he admitted how silly that was, he knew it was nonetheless true.

Four.

Three.

Two.

One.

"And so," said Declan Sage, "that's the story of how the good people of the Village of Reek were saved."

The only other person on the subway platform was a tall elf with green hair. The old man had been talking for a long time—maybe the trains stopped running at eleven or something? The elf checked his watch.

"The Chosen One reunited two worlds," Declan Sage continued, "and delivered us from the Great Dragon, and broke Nimue's wicked spell."

The elf gave the old man a dollar, because it seemed like the thing to do.

"What's your name, son?"

"Mossblossom," said the elf. He winced. "I'm . . . thinking of changing it. So, now . . . *who* was the Chosen One, exactly? Was it Scott, or John or Merlin? Or Emily, for that matter?"

Declan Sage was chuckling and shaking his head.

"My son," he said, "the answer to that mystery is a story that will have to wait for another time."

He smiled absently. Mossblossom frowned.

"You have no idea, do you."

"No."

A MAGICALLY DELICIOUS TRILOGY. *

*Contains your recommended daily allowance of adventure, magic, and humor.